Tracy swallowed au
She wasn't going to

Especially since she'd so obviously enjoyed his kiss.
And because she desperately wanted his trust.
"I didn't want my purpose for being here, my wish to
know Seth, to get tangled up in what I was feeling
toward you."

"And I didn't want my desire for you to cloud my
judgment of your purpose. But you showed me
today—" he whispered as he trailed kisses along
the line of her jaw and throat "—that you have an
incredible core of strength. No matter how fragile...
your appearance, you proved...you are no pushover."

Though his compliment warmed her heart, her gut
tightened. She squeezed her eyes closed, feeling
like a fraud. "I didn't feel strong," she admitted.
"I felt horribly vulnerable." She tightened her grip
around his shoulders as the chilling horror of those
moments washed through her again. She buried
her head under his chin, her ear pressed to his
breastbone and shivered. "I did what I had to to
protect Seth, but...I was scared to death."

* * *

Be sure to check out the next books in
The Coltons of Oklahoma miniseries.
The Coltons of Oklahoma:
Family secrets always find a way to resurface...

* * *

If you're on Twitter, tell us what you think of
Harlequin Romantic Suspense!
#harlequinromsuspense

Dear Reader,

I've been lucky enough over the years to be a part of several Colton continuities. I love this family and am thrilled to kick off the latest chapter in their saga! John "Big J" Colton is the patriarch of a large, successful ranching family in Oklahoma. At the Lucky C ranch, Big J's children—five sons and one daughter—will face their share of danger, buried secrets and personal challenges on their way to romantic happily-ever-afters!

First up is Jack Colton, the oldest son and divorced father to a precocious five-year-old son. Jack is highly protective of his little boy, especially when Tracy McCain, a relative of his late ex-wife, shows up wanting to build a relationship with his boy. Jack's son is Tracy's only family, and she craves the link to her recently deceased cousin. Though Jack is wary of Tracy's motives, he can't deny his attraction to her. Nor can he ignore his instinct to protect her, especially when it becomes clear some unknown threat has followed her to the Lucky C ranch.

I hope you enjoy *Colton Cowboy Protector*. I had a blast writing Jack and Tracy's precarious journey on the way to true love. Enjoy!

Best wishes and happy reading,

Beth Cornelison

COLTON COWBOY
PROTECTOR

Beth Cornelison

HARLEQUIN® ROMANTIC SUSPENSE

Special thanks and acknowledgment are given to Beth Cornelison
for her contribution to the The Coltons of Oklahoma miniseries.

Recycling programs
for this product may
not exist in your area.

ISBN-13: 978-0-373-27921-0

Colton Cowboy Protector

Copyright © 2015 by Harlequin Books S.A.

Printed in U.S.A.

Beth Cornelison started writing stories as a child when she penned a tale about the adventures of her cat, Ajax. A Georgia native, she received her bachelor's degree in public relations from the University of Georgia. After working in public relations for a little more than a year, she moved with her husband to Louisiana, where she decided to pursue her love of writing fiction.

Since that first time, Beth has written many more stories of adventure and romantic suspense and has won numerous honors for her work, including a coveted Golden Heart Award in romantic suspense from Romance Writers of America. She is active on the board of directors for the North Louisiana Storytellers and Authors of Romance (NOLA STARS) and loves reading, traveling, *Peanuts'* Snoopy and spending downtime with her family.

She writes from her home in Louisiana, where she lives with her husband, one son and two cats who think they are people. Beth loves to hear from her readers. You can write to her at PO Box 5418, Bossier City, LA 71171, or visit her website, bethcornelison.com.

Books by Beth Cornelison

HARLEQUIN ROMANTIC SUSPENSE

Visit Beth Cornelison's profile page
at Harlequin.com for more titles.

To my family, the whole loving, supportive,
often goofy bunch of you!

Thank you to Deborah Boyd, who won the
chance to have her kitty Oh La La Sleek (Sleekie)
memorialized in this book through the
Brenda Novak Auction for the Cure.

Prologue

The man reminded her of a wolf. His pale eyes held a feral quality, his heavily graying black hair was shaggy and thick, and his thin, sloped nose brought to mind a canine muzzle. She shivered as he slid into the front seat next to her, but his wild appearance boded well. She needed him to be the deadly predator he resembled. The two-faced mouse that had ruined her life and stolen her child from her needed to pay.

They'd parked in the farthest corner of the parking lot outside the range of the security cameras. She knew the spot was safe, because she'd checked the surveillance tapes herself. As it was after hours, few cars were left in the lot, and darkness added another layer of cover.

She slid the wolf man a file and gave him a hard stare. "I hired you because I was told you're the best. Naturally, discretion is of utmost importance. This can't be traced back to me or my husband."

"Naturally," he deadpanned. He reached into his front shirt pocket and pulled out a pack of cigarettes. Tapping one out, he flicked a silver lighter and lit his smoke. The tip glowed red like an evil eye in the dark.

She balled her hands in her lap, watching him uneasily as he flipped through the file. "I'll want proof when the job is complete."

Blowing smoke after her, he sent her a snide look, as if her request was beneath him. "I'll finish the job."

"Be sure you do. You don't get the last of your fee until I know that she's paid for what she did to my son."

He slapped the file shut and curled his lip in a sneer that revealed a lupine-like incisor. "Oh, she'll pay. Your son was my friend, my partner in a deal that went south when he died. I lost a small fortune. This job is personal. I won't rest until his death is avenged and that backstabbing bitch is dead."

Chapter 1

"In one hundred feet, turn right onto access road," the stilted voice of the rental car's GPS intoned.

With a deep breath for courage, Tracy McCain signaled the turn. She noted with interest that the car ahead of her on the isolated stretch of rural Oklahoma highway also made a right onto the side road leading to the sprawling ranch of cattleman John "Big J" Colton.

More interesting were the three cars that followed her onto the long driveway, including a television news van complete with a satellite dish on top. What the heck was going on at the Lucky C ranch today?

The iron gates, normally requiring someone at the main house to buzz you in, stood agape, allowing the parade of cars to continue up to the house unimpeded. As Tracy passed through the stone-walled entry, she noticed the Lucky C logo, an upright, good-luck horseshoe with a C inside, atop the posts on either side of the iron gate.

She hoped the logo boded well for her. She could use a bit of good luck today for her mission. From what her cousin had told her, the Coltons were a stubborn bunch, hard-nosed and highly protective of their family and their business.

Tracy wiped her sweaty palms on the legs of her slacks as the string of vehicles rolled closer to the ranch buildings, past acre upon acre of prime grazing fields. She looked for a place to pull off and park as they approached the main house, but, trapped between the SUV in front of her and the news van behind her, she had no real choice but to pull right up the drive to the front door of the Colton mansion. Laura had told her the Coltons were wealthy, but the glorious estate before her sent a fresh roll of trepidation through her. Holy cow—or maybe she should say holy *cowboy*—the place was big...and beautiful.

She knew how David must have felt going up against Goliath. What were the odds that she, an unemployed widow, a down-on-her-luck nobody with only a tenuous right to the claim she wanted to stake, could hold sway with the mighty Coltons?

She glanced at the snapshot of a small boy that she'd laid on the passenger seat, and her spirits lifted. Seth was worth the effort. And she owed Laura. Big time.

When the line of cars stopped on the cobbled drive in front of the stone-facade mansion, a man in a white button-down shirt and black pants yanked open her driver-side door.

Tracy gasped and shrank away as he stuck a hand toward her. "Wh-what are you doing?"

He flashed a lopsided grin. "Offering you a hand out. We cowboys are raised to be helpful to ladies."

"Oh…thanks, but no." She glanced around at the mani-cured lawn. "Where should I park?"

"You don't."

She jerked a startled look back to the dark-haired man, who either had a head start on his summer tan or an en-viable heritage lending him his copper-toned skin. "Par-don?"

Had she been recognized as an interloper? Was she being dismissed even without getting to state her case?

The cowboy chuckled and wiggled his fingers, indi-cating she should get out of the car. "Parking is my job today. But don't worry. I drive cars as well as I drive cattle. I won't scratch it."

A car horn blasted behind her, and another man in a white shirt leaned out of a vehicle behind her and shouted, "Come on, Daniel. Schmooze the ladies on your own time, man. You're holding up the line!"

The cowboy-valet at her door smiled at his cohort and deliberately scratched his temple with his middle finger. Offering his hand to her again, he said, "Ma'am."

With a nervous grin, she grabbed her purse off the floor and took his callused hand to slip out of the rental car. As the valet—Daniel, the other man had called him—climbed behind the wheel, she remembered her messenger bag. "Wait! I need that."

She pointed past him to the passenger seat. But in-stead of the bag, he zeroed in on her snapshot. He picked up the photo with a curious frown. "Hey, isn't this—?"

She snatched the picture, drawing a deeper scowl from him. "My bag. Please."

Daniel retrieved the satchel and handed it to her, along with a small piece of paper. "Write your tag number on this and give it to whoever's manning the front door when you're ready to leave. Someone will bring your car around."

With that, he closed the door and sped away.

"But I don't know—" She quickly shifted her attention to the rental car's license plate and caught the first few digits before her valet-cowboy turned out of the circular drive and headed toward the back of the property. As she crossed the driveway, headed for the front door, she stuck the photo in her purse, then fumbled for a pen to write the plate numbers down.

Tracy joined the stylishly dressed reporter and bored-looking cameraman from the news station, climbing the decorative concrete steps to the front door. The reporter knocked on the dark wood door inset with an ornate glass window. While they waited for an answer, Tracy practiced in her head what she would say when she confronted her cousin's ex. Honesty was a good policy, but how open would the Coltons be to her proposal, if they knew her past? She didn't have long to mull over the question, as the door was answered quickly by an effusive older woman with a dark bob.

"Veronica Hamm, KRQY News," the reporter said, offering her hand.

"Of course! I'd know that pretty face anywhere!" the woman at the door gushed, ignoring the proffered hand and swooping in for a girlie hug and air kisses on each cheek. "Come in, come in! I'm Abra Colton. Thank you for coming."

Tracy's stomach flip-flopped. *Abra Colton. Seth's grandmother.* As matriarch of the Colton clan, Abra could be key to whether Tracy was accepted by the family or not.

Their hostess waved the cameraman and Tracy through the door without so much as a "hello." Abra clearly had use only for the newswoman, and she continued buzzing over her like a bee to the sweetest rose. "The media room is to the right at the back. We'll have our big announcement in just a little while." She hooked arms with Veronica, ignoring Tracy and the cameraman as she walked the reporter into the house. "In the meantime, help yourself to the buffet out by the pool, and a glass of champagne. Big J and I ordered cases of the best bubbly from France for the occasion!"

As the cameraman trailed after Abra and Veronica like an obedient puppy, Tracy lingered awkwardly in the entry hall. She glanced around at the high ceilings, marble floors and triple arches leading into the formal living room, and her pulse picked up speed.

How had Laura walked away from all this grandeur and wealth? Seth clearly had a better life here than what she could have offered, but leaving her son behind had been harder on Laura than she pretended to the Coltons. She'd done what she had because she'd wanted the security and opportunity that a life with his father could afford Seth.

"A little less ogling and a little more giddy-up if you don't want to get separated from the rest of your crew."

Tracy gasped and spun to face the man who'd spoken. She found herself staring up into the bright green eyes of a cowboy with broad shoulders, shaggy chestnut hair and a somewhat surly expression.

Her mouth dried as she held his level stare. He had the rugged good looks Laura had said the Colton men all shared, and a commanding presence that made Tracy's toes curl in feminine appreciation, despite his less than welcoming greeting.

"I'm, um...not with the news crew."

Tall, Dark and Sullen grunted. "In that case, the food

is out by the pool. Eat up, 'cause your hostess spent as
much on that buffet as two pure-blood, registered breeding bulls would cost at auction." With that, he strode
away, his gait brisk and confident, and disappeared into
the crowd of guests.

When the doorbell sounded a few seconds later, Tracy
was still standing in the foyer, gaping at the spot in the
mingling crowd where the devilishly handsome but curt
cowboy had joined the soirée. A woman wearing a housekeeper's uniform and her silver hair twisted up in a bun
scurried out from a side door and balked when she saw
Tracy.

"For Pete's sake, don't just stand there, girl!" The older
woman flapped her thin hands as if to shoo her out of
the entry hall. "There are guests to serve and drinks to
be poured. Get busy! Don't make me report you to the
catering company."

Tracy gave a self-conscious chuckle. "I'm not with the
caterers. I'm looking for—"

The woman jostled her out of the way to open the front
door. Tracy's opportunity to ask for directions was lost
as the housekeeper greeted the arriving guests with en-
thusiastic smiles and hospitality.

Rather than continue to stand at the door like a bump
on a log, Tracy sidled into the living room. She clutched
her messenger bag close to her body to avoid jostling anyone or knocking over one of the numerous champagne
flutes resting on trays in the exquisitely furnished room.
Dressed in basic khakis and a simple print blouse the
same caramel color as her hair, she noted that she was
underdressed for whatever event the Coltons were cel-
ebrating. Feeling all the more out of place, and hoping
to camouflage herself against the French-vanilla walls,
she began inching her way through the clusters of guests.

Maybe she should just leave. Clearly, now was not the time to approach Jack. She was an uninvited interloper at a high-society event. She didn't belong. Story of her life.

Sighing with resignation, she'd started weaving her way back toward the front door when a large, boisterous man with a thick shock of silver hair caught her arm. "Hey, little darlin'. Whatcha doin'?"

Busted.

"I—I'm sorry. I was just leaving…"

"Leaving? Hell, darlin', the party's just getting started good."

She recognized the green eyes that flashed at her with mirth. Tall, Dark and Surly's eyes had mesmerized her with the same bright emerald shade, and the gruff cowboy could be this flirtatious gentleman in thirty years… if he added this man's playful smile.

"Why is your hand empty? You should have a glass of bubbly. This is a celebration, darlin'!" He snagged a glass of champagne off a passing tray and shoved it at her. "Bottoms up!"

"Oh, I'm not—" She stopped short as she realized who this animated man was. She'd seen his picture when she'd researched the Lucky C on Google before coming to Oklahoma. "You're Big J! I mean…J-John Colton."

Though John laughed and nodded amiably, she felt her cheeks heat with embarrassment. Great. She'd just called one of the wealthiest and most powerful men in the ranching industry—heck, in all of the United States' agribusiness—by his nickname. *Way to make a good first impression…*

"Yes, I am, darlin'. Yes, I am." He took a step back and gave her a slow once-over that brought the stinging flush back to her cheeks. "And who might you be? I believe I'd remember meeting you, if I'd ever had the pleasure."

"Tracy McCain. I'm actually here to speak to Jack. Can you point me toward him?"

"I could, but…I'm still enjoying your company." The older man winked. "Besides, Jack is probably hiding somewhere until time for the announcement."

"Announcement?"

Big J gave her a you've-got-to-be-kidding look. "Greta's engagement. That's why we're all here lifting a glass."

"Oh." Tracy fumbled for anything Laura might have told her about Greta.

But Big J seemed oblivious to her mental catch-up and helped her out by adding, "It's not every day a daddy gets to toast his only daughter getting hitched, so we went all out for my Greta."

Only daughter…of course. Greta was Jack's sister. The youngest of the Colton children. Tracy smiled and raised the glass John had foisted on her. "Well, here's to Greta."

"To Greta!" Big J clinked his glass with hers, so hard the contents of both drinks sloshed out.

Without warning, he gave a shrill whistle, startling Tracy so much that a shot of adrenaline raced through her, tripping her pulse.

"Brett! C'mere, son." Big J waved someone over, and a tall, athletic-looking man with short brown hair separated himself from a circle of cloying women and strutted across the room.

Tracy goggled as he approached. Dear God, did the Coltons have an account at hunkycowboys.com? She had yet to meet one who didn't look as if he'd walked off the pages of a hot-ranch-hands catalog.

Big J put his hand on Brett's shoulder when he reached them, and jerked his glass toward Tracy. "Brett, my boy. This lovely filly is Tracy McCann."

"Um…McCain."

"I am going to leave her in your good hands," Big J continued, as if he hadn't heard her correction. "She's looking for Jack. But before she talks to your brother, I think she needs something to eat."

"No, really, I'm not here to eat. I just need to speak to Jack." Tracy's stomach chose that inopportune moment to growl. Thankfully, the din of the party conversation and background country music muffled the sound.

Brett took her hand and, rather than shaking it, merely left his fingers wrapped warmly around hers as he gave her a smile that twinkled in his trademark Colton-green eyes. "My dad's right. You don't want to meet my brother on an empty stomach. Besides, the brisket is so tender it will melt in your mouth. Follow me."

He tugged her hand as he led the way out to the pool, where a small acoustic band was playing the country tunes she'd heard inside. Brett steered her to a buffet table piled high with beef brisket, rolls, fresh fruit, veggies and dips, cheeses of all types, and an array of the most sumptuous-looking desserts Tracy had ever seen. Her mouth watered, and she decided it would be a good idea to have at least a *little* something to eat. She and Brett both picked up plates and started down the buffet. "Wow!"

He chuckled. "I know, right? Abra knows how to put out a spread, huh?" He used the tongs from a tray of cheeses to pile sliced beef and bite-size meat pastries onto Tracy's plate. When melodic laughter drifted to them from a small group by the desserts, he called, "Hey, Ryan, save some of those brownies for the rest of us."

"You snooze, you lose," a muscular man with telltale green eyes marking him as another Colton quipped. "Greta said I could have hers."

The brunette woman beside Ryan elbowed him. "I said you could have mine, not the rest of the tray!"

Brett hitched his head toward the group. "Tracy, have you met this crew? My brother, Detective Ryan Colton of the Tulsa PD, and of course, the honorees, my baby sister, Greta, and her fiancé, Mark You-Better-Be-Good-to-Her-or-I'll-Kick-Your-Ass Stanton."

The russet-haired man next to Greta laughed as he offered his hand to Tracy. Brett's face sobered, and he gave Mark a squinty-eyed glare. "I'm not joking, man."

Greta shoved her brother's shoulder. "Brett, stop trying to intimidate my fiancé, you big goof."

Brett grinned broadly. "Yeah, okay." But when Mark smiled in relief, Brett blanked his face again in an instant and raised an eyebrow. "But I mean it."

"I already warned Mark that I know a hundred ways to kill a man and hide the body without being caught," Ryan deadpanned.

Tracy gave Mark a sympathetic look. "Tough gig, marrying into a family with this much testosterone."

"Yeah," Mark said with a sappy grin as he kissed his fiancée's temple, "but Greta's worth it."

Brett made a gagging noise, then flinched as a cold jet of water spritzed them all.

Tracy heard a youthful giggle as Brett spun around with a playful growl. She leaned to her left to see who was behind him and spotted a familiar-looking little boy with a water gun.

Her heart seized. *Seth.*

She gaped at the boy who so obviously resembled his paternal family, and a knot of emotion clogged her throat. Seeing her cousin's son, her only living family, in the flesh for the first time was no less poignant in this setting than if she'd been greeting him five years ago when he was a newborn in the hospital nursery.

"All right, pal. You asked for it!" Brett said, sweeping him up and over his shoulder.

Seth's laughter rang over the party sounds as Brett took three long steps to the deep end of the swimming pool and tossed his nephew in, clothes and all.

Tracy gasped and took a step toward the pool, prepared to dive in after Seth if needed. But the little boy broke the surface of the water, still grinning from ear to ear and clutching his water gun. He swam skillfully to the ladder to climb out, calling, "Okay, Uncle Brett, this is war!"

Brett grinned as his nephew shook his wet hair. "Bring it on, Seth. I'm ready for you, buddy."

Seth aimed his gun and blasted Brett and several other guests with a jet of cold water. Tracy bit her bottom lip to cover a smile.

Abra strode briskly through the French doors, clearly not amused. She clattered out onto the patio, her high heels clicking on the concrete, and gave Brett a stern frown. "The two of you cut that out at once! I'll not have you ruining Greta's party," she said, barely keeping her tone above a hiss. She quickly schooled her face and smiled at her guests. "I'm so sorry for my grandson's behavior. He can be rather a handful sometimes."

Tracy bristled, ready to fly to Seth's defense, just as Greta touched her arm and spoke to her. "So, Tracy, are you a friend of Mark's?" She divided a curious look between Tracy and her fiancé.

Mark shook his head, at the same time that Tracy said, "Um…actually, I'm not here for the party. I came to see Jack. On a personal matter."

Greta's eyes widened, and she sent Ryan a knowing look that said, *Well, well...interesting.*

Tracy's cheeks flamed again, and she cleared her throat. "Could you point me toward him, please?"

Greta blinked. "You don't know what he looks like?"

"Well, no. I mean, based on the Coltons I've met so far today, I'm assuming he's green-eyed, dark-haired and gorgeous, but beyond that..."

An amused grin tugged the corner of Ryan's mouth, and he sent a glance around the area, using his advantageous height to see over the heads of the assembled guests. With the glass in his hand, he motioned to the far side of the pool. "That's him over there, wrapping Seth up in the towel."

Tracy turned to look, and her breath caught. The man draping Seth in a beach towel was none other than the cowboy she'd encountered in the foyer. Mr. Tall, Dark and Surly himself.

Chapter 2

With his gaze, Jack Colton followed the sounds of splashing water and his son's playful laugh to the swimming pool and cracked a small grin. Seth's carefree, sometimes mischievous nature reminded him of himself when he was younger, before life, fatherhood and the demands of a large cattle ranch replaced his wild ways with a more responsible attitude. The mirthful sounds were silenced by a rebuke from Jack's mother, and he tensed.

Wasn't it bad enough that Abra was putting on this dog-and-pony show, flaunting Greta's engagement to the world in order to boost her own social standing? The media was here, for cripes' sake! Not that Jack wasn't happy for his sister. Greta's engagement deserved to be toasted and celebrated. Just not so publicly. This spectacle was an embarrassment.

Jack strode quickly to the pool to retrieve his son, noting that Brett had been the one egging the boy on. Jack appreciated the rapport his brother had with five-year-old Seth, but not when it led his son down the wrong path... namely one that crossed Abra's.

"Seth," Jack said calmly, but with a tone and volume that brooked no resistance. His son glanced up, and Jack gave a subtle head jerk. As Seth obediently scurried out of the water, Jack turned his gaze to Brett and sent him a false smile. "Thanks."

His brother held up both hands, laughing, "He started it."

"Yeah, but you're an adult. Act like one."

Brett gave him a who-whizzed-in-your-Wheaties look and turned to join the conversation behind him. No doubt ragging on his grumpy big brother. When had Jack become such a grandpa?

Jack dragged a hand over his mouth and sighed. He was feeling edgy today, and it wasn't Brett's fault. This lavish party—$20,000 for champagne?—chafed his practical business sense. Anything frivolous that ate away the bottom line was a burr under his saddle. This party was the whole prickly bush. Grunting in frustration, he swiped a beach towel off a lounge chair and held it out for Seth.

"Sorry, Daddy," Seth said mournfully, his eyes downcast as he slopped over in his wet clothes and shoes.

"Didn't I ask you this morning to be on your best behavior?" Squatting, Jack wrapped the towel around him and rubbed an end over his shaggy brown hair.

"Yes, sir." Seth lifted a rebellious look. "But this party is so *boring*! There are no kids to play with and no bouncy castle or games."

Jack was bored, too, and eager to get out in the north pasture to check on the most recently born calves. "Tell you what. Go change into dry clothes, behave like the good boy I know you can be for the rest of the party and we'll get ice cream in town tonight. Deal?"

Seth's face brightened. "Two scoops?"

Jack raised an eyebrow. "A wheeler-dealer like your grandpa, I see."

Seth grinned at the comparison. "Pa Pa says, 'never take the first offer. Always ask for a more better deal.'"

"Just 'better.' Not 'more better.'"

Seth wrinkled his nose. "Huh?"

Inside the house, Seth's Pa Pa, Big J, gave a bellowing laugh that reached all the way to the pool. Jack shook his head. Seth could do worse than to emulate Big J. Poor grammar aside.

"Sure. Two scoops. If you eat a good dinner." Great, now Jack sounded like someone's mother. Not *his* mother, though. Abra had never cared whether he ate his vegetables or brushed his teeth. She still barely bothered herself with her children, unless it served her purposes. Case in point, Greta's engagement party.

"Excuse me."

Jack angled his head to meet the gaze of the woman beside him who'd spoken. He squinted against the bright Oklahoma sun, which backlit her.

"Are you Jack Colton?" she asked.

"I am."

"May I have a word with you?" Her voice was noticeably thin and unsteady. She cleared her throat and added, "Privately?"

In his head, Jack groaned. What now?

He swatted Seth on the bottom. "Go get changed, Spud."

With a curious glance at the woman, Seth nodded and squished across the lawn toward the old ranch house.

Jack pushed to his feet, his knee cracking thanks to

an old rodeo injury, and faced the woman at eye level. Well, almost eye level. Though tall for a woman, she was still a good five or six inches shorter than his six foot one. He recognized her as the woman he'd seen earlier lurking in the foyer, practically casing the main house. "And you are…?"

He suspected she was a reporter, based on the messenger bag hanging from her shoulder, though why a reporter would need to speak privately with him was beyond him. He had nothing to say to any reporter, privately or otherwise.

She took a deep breath and nervously wet her lips. "Tracy McCain."

The name didn't ring any bells, but when she extended her hand in greeting, he shook it.

She added a shy smile, her porcelain cheeks flushing, and a stir of attraction tickled Jack deep inside. Hell, more than a stir. He gave her a leisurely scrutiny, sizing her up. She might be tall and thin, but she still had womanly curves to go with her delicate china-doll face. "Am I supposed to know you?"

Her smile dropped. "Laura never mentioned me?"

His ex-wife's name instantly raised his hackles and his defenses. His eyes narrowed. "Not that I recall. How do you know Laura?"

"I'm her cousin. Her maternal aunt's daughter. From Colorado Springs."

Jack gritted his back teeth. Laura had been dead only a few months and already relations she'd never mentioned were crawling out of the woodwork like roaches after the light's turned off. The allure of the Colton wealth had attracted more than one gold-digging pest over the years. "You should know, Laura signed an agreement when we divorced. She got a tidy settlement in place of any alimony. The agreement meant she gave up any further financial claim on Colton money or the Lucky C."

Tracy lifted her chin. "I'm aware."

"So you're barking up the wrong tree, if you're looking for cash."

Tracy blinked her pale blue eyes, and her expression shifted, hardened. "I'm not after money," she said, with frost in her tone.

Jack scratched his chin and tipped his head, giving her a skeptical glare. "Then what?"

She waved a hand toward the house, then, as if realizing they'd have no more privacy inside than here by the pool, she frowned. "Is there someplace quiet we can talk?"

Ten minutes ago, Jack had been dying for an excuse to ditch Abra's party. Now he had the excuse he'd been looking for, but his gut told him he'd be no better off hearing Miss Blue Eyes out.

"Fine." He huffed an exasperated sigh and headed across the lawn, leaving her to follow or not. Her choice.

The main house was a good distance from the stable, barn, bunkhouse and other outbuildings— two miles by the dirt road, a little less if you cut across fields and grassy lawns. He had driven one of the ranch's utility vehicles over to the party, but some peevish rebellion in him decided to walk now. If Tracy wanted to talk to him, she could hoof it to the stable. Ninety-five degree Oklahoma heat and gravel road be damned.

He walked too quickly for her to match his long-legged stride, but to her credit, she didn't fall too far behind. As they neared the stable, cutting across a corner of one of the holding pens, he aimed a finger at one of the many cow patties, warning, "Watch your step."

She drew a quick breath and took a last-minute side

step to avoid a pile. For what it was worth. Her modest brown dress pumps were caked in mud, the heels likely ruined by the gravel. Jack experienced a moment of compunction for her destroyed shoes, but he pushed it aside. She should have known better than to wear shoes like that to a ranch.

He wiped sweat from his brow as he entered the shade of the stable, where large fans circulated the scents of manure, straw and leather in the stuffy alley between horse stalls. In a shady corner of an empty stall, their black barn cat, Sleek, napped between hunting expeditions. The family wanted Sleek to catch mice, which she did, but the feline seemed more interested in birds…and sneaking into the old ranch house to sleep on Seth's bed when Jack wasn't looking.

Jack gave a pat to one of the mares, which stuck her nose out as he passed, then made his way to Buck's stall. His buckskin gelding tossed his black mane when Jack opened the stall door and led him out.

When Tracy caught up to him, she was breathing heavily and perspiration rolled down her face and neck. The fine, sweat-dampened hair around her temples and ears curled in sweet golden ringlets, and over the musty smell of the stable, a floral scent wafted to him with the fan's breeze. The sweet aroma was completely out of place here, much like the woman wearing the perfume, and the heady scent made lust curl in his belly. Her stylish khaki slacks and simple print blouse were more suited to a boardroom than a tack room, and Tracy's knitted brow as she scanned the horse stalls spoke for her uneasiness on his turf.

He took a currycomb from a shelf and started grooming Buck. "You wanted privacy, you got it. So talk."

She let the messenger bag slide off her arm and thud

onto a nearby bench. "There wasn't anyplace…closer?" she panted.

He shrugged. "Sure there was. But I figured if I could groom ole Buck while we talked, I could get a jump on my to-do list for the day."

And if he kept himself busy combing Buck, maybe he wouldn't be as easily distracted by her lush lips and doe-like blue eyes. Her fragile, china-doll appearance made her seem vulnerable, and until he knew what she was after, Jack didn't want to feel any weakness or sympathy toward her.

She dabbed ineffectually at her damp cheeks and brow, then flapped the front of her blouse, trying to cool down. "Okay, so…I wanted to talk about Seth."

Jack tensed, his gut filling with acid. He squeezed the currycomb with a death grip and grated, "No."

"I… What do you mean, no? You haven't even heard what I want to—"

"I don't need to hear. My son is off-limits. Nonnegotiable." With an effort, Jack loosened his grip on the currycomb and continued stroking Buck's beige hide.

Tracy was silent for a moment, shifting her weight and swatting at a horsefly that was as drawn to her perfume as Jack was.

"All I want is the opportunity to get to know my cousin's son. I want Seth to know things about Laura that he might not know."

Jack shook his head and aimed the currycomb at Tracy. "He knows all he needs to know, and I won't have you filling his head with information that will lead to questions best left alone, or truths about his mother that will only hurt him."

Tracy straightened her spine, her expression affronted.

"I have no intention of hurting him. I… What would I say about his mother that would hurt Seth?"

"The truth. She abandoned him when he was a baby."

"Abandoned?" Tracy chuffed a humorless laugh. "She did no such thing!"

Jack paused from the grooming to face her, cocking his head. "Really? What would you call it?"

"Laura loved Seth!" Tracy clapped a hand to her chest, pleading her case with wide, earnest eyes. "She did what she thought was best for him. She saw that he'd have a better life here on the Lucky C with you and your family than she could give him as an unemployed single mother. She never forgot a birthday, always sent Christmas presents—"

He scoffed. "You can't buy a kid's affection. Presents are no substitute for being there."

"I know that. And…so did she." Tracy looked at the ground as she said the last, not sounding at all sure of her claim.

"Doesn't matter. I didn't give him her gifts or cards."

Tracy's chin jerked up. "What? Why not?"

"It would have only confused him."

Now she tilted her head to the side, her eyes suspicious. "Confused him why?"

"I told Seth his mother died when he was a baby."

Tracy gasped in outrage.

Jack turned back to Buck and patted the gelding's neck. "I thought that would be easier for him to handle than knowing she chose to walk away."

"She didn't— You shouldn't—" Tracy sputtered. "You had as much to do with her leaving as she did! You knew she wasn't suited to ranch life. You encouraged her to go her own way when you saw how unhappy she was."

Jack gritted his back teeth, feeling a knot in his stomach. The failure of his marriage was the last thing he wanted to rehash today…or ever. Seth was the only good thing that came out of his years with Laura. He took a slow breath and swallowed the bitter taste at the back of his throat. "Water under the bridge," he said in a low, even tone.

He raised the currycomb to continue his work, but Tracy strode over and caught his wrist. "Would you stop that long enough to hear me out? My cousin was not the monster you're making her out to be!"

He heaved a put-upon sigh and tossed the currycomb aside. "No one said she was a monster," he said under his breath. Then, only a little louder, he added, "I wouldn't have married her if she were a monster. She had her good points, and at one time, I thought I loved her."

He angled a look over his shoulder at Tracy. She was swiping at the sweat on her face with her wrist, her pale skin flushed from the heat. He stepped over to the shelf where he kept his personal tack equipment and fished a bandanna out of his saddlebag. He held it out to her, and she eyed it suspiciously. "It's clean. I promise."

With a murmured thank-you, she dried her face and neck, and ambled closer to a fan so the current of air blew in her face. "As I was saying…I want the chance to spend time with Seth, to get to know him. After Laura died, I promised her…" Tracy paused and swallowed hard. To his dismay, Jack thought he saw tears fill her eyes. God, no tears! Please! He hated seeing a woman cry. Tears were worse than splinters under his fingernails, and he'd do anything to avoid them.

After a slow breath, Tracy seemed more composed—thank the Lord—and continued. "I promised Laura that I would make sure her son knew how much she loved him, the kind of woman she was and everything she did for me. She deserves that."

Jack folded his arms over his chest and leaned against a wall. "What she did for you?"

Tracy nodded. "The day of the car accident that killed her…"

"Yeah?"

"…she was helping me. I was in the car with her when she died. She'd saved me from a really bad situation, helped me escape…" Tracy wet her lips and glanced away for a moment before continuing. "The man who ran us off the road was my husband."

Clenching his jaw, Jack recalled what he'd been told about the accident. "He was arrested for vehicular manslaughter. Right?"

She nodded.

"So he's in jail now?"

"He was. But…he was shanked the second night he was in jail and died on the way to the hospital."

Jack arched one eyebrow. He hadn't known that tidbit. "I'm sorry."

A sad smile tugged the corner of her mouth. "I'm not."

Jack stared at her. Read between the lines. "He abused you." It was a statement, not a question. Abuse would explain a lot of the vulnerability he sensed with her.

She said nothing for a minute. Finally, her shoulders slumped, and she nodded. "Verbally. Mentally. He was spiteful and mean. Loved making me cry for sport."

Jack felt a hot ball of rage well in his gut toward the man.

"He only hit me once, though."

Jack barked a laugh of disbelief. "Just once?"

Her eyes rounded, and she took a step back. "Y-yeah."

"As if that makes it all right or wins him points?" He drilled a finger at her. "Once is one time too many."

Her hand fluttered to her throat, where she dabbed again at the sweat collecting there. "I agree. But my point is…I owe Laura. I know how much Seth meant to her and how much it would mean to her—how much it would mean to *me*—if I could spend some time with her son."

Jack rubbed the bridge of his nose. "For what purpose? So he can have another woman walk out of his life in a few days?"

"Who said I wanted to walk out? I don't have a child of my own. Maybe I'm looking for something long-term, something permanent."

Ice slid through Jack's blood, and he lurched away from the wall. "Excuse me?"

Tracy blinked, confused. "I said I wouldn't walk out on him. I want—"

"If you're looking to sue for custody or visitation rights, you should know that the divorce agreement Laura signed denies her *or her family* the right to come back here and try to take Seth from me."

Jack stalked toward Tracy until she'd backed against the far alley wall, and he loomed over her. "Seth is mine. All mine. I have sole custody, and that's how it's gonna stay."

She hunched her shoulders, trying to make herself smaller, and he realized how his power play must have appeared to her. Intimidating, threatening, hostile… Okay, he had meant to intimidate her and drive home his point. But he'd forgotten for a moment how that tactic would play with an abused woman. Damn it!

He eased back a step, giving her breathing room, while still making his point that he was unyielding on the question of custody. He would fight her to his last dollar to keep his son. When he drew a calming lungful of air, he inhaled the sweet scent of her. Heat unrelated to the summer temperatures skittered through him. His pulse kicked harder as he imagined what it might be like to pin her against the wall and kiss her full, frowning lips. Standing this close to her, he could see her chin quiver and hear the agitated rasp of her breathing. Damn the man who'd scarred her psyche this way! And damn himself for finding Tracy so alluring, so sweetly sexy and begging for protection.

He was far more likely to need protection from her and her plans for Seth than she needed protecting.

"I don't want to take him from you." Her voice trembled, and when she raised her gaze, he saw moisture in her eyes. But also defiance. "I don't want to be at odds with you on this matter but...if I have to go to court to win the right to see Seth—" her throat convulsed as she swallowed "—I will."

Chapter 3

After Tracy threw down the gauntlet regarding visitation with Seth, Jack hustled her back to the party, driving one of the MULE side x sides this time, and ordered her off the ranch. He'd not have any relative of his ex-wife blackmailing him into visitations with Seth. Especially not if those visits included the possibility of Seth hearing upsetting truths about his mother. Or if said visits could lead to an attempt for shared custody. Or...*cripes*, the possibilities chilled Jack.

He let Tracy out at the pool area and directed her to leave immediately, before he moved the MULE to the edge of the lawn. When he returned to the party to look for Seth, he spotted Brett near the buffet line, yukking it up with some slick-looking customers in Stetsons too clean and crease-free to be real cowboys. Brett caught his eye and waved him over.

Seeing no graceful way out, Jack crossed the lawn

and gave the men with his brother a half smile as he approached. He could smell big-city investors and rancher wannabes from a mile away. These guys reeked of money and little practical ranching knowledge.

"Jack, I'd like you to meet some gentlemen. Bill and George here are from Dallas and are interested in helping us get started in horse breeding."

Nailed it. Jack gloated silently as he shook the men's hands.

"I've been telling them how I found that stud in OKC with papers and a great bloodline."

Jack lifted one eyebrow. "What stud?"

"I told you about him when I talked to you last week about my idea for breeding cutting horses."

Drawing a slow breath, Jack pinned his brother with a level stare. "As I recall, I told you we weren't making any changes to the business plan for the ranch. I have no interest in breeding cutting horses."

Brett gave the businessmen an awkward grin. "Well, yeah, but *I'm* interested, and so is Daniel. I've been looking into it, and George here says he has connections that can—"

Jack took his brother's arm and pulled him aside. "Excuse us for a minute, gentlemen."

Brett muttered a curse under his breath and glared at Jack. "Don't blow this for us, man. You know Daniel is looking to set up his own breeding program, and if the Lucky C doesn't provide him with the resources, he'll take his talents, and his profits, elsewhere."

"If he wants to leave the ranch, he should."

Brett scowled and angled his head. "You don't mean that. He's family! He belongs at the Lucky C. That means giving him reason to stay here, and Geronimo is a fantastic reason."

Jack exhaled slowly and shoved his hands in his back pockets. "He only belongs here if he wants to stay. I won't be party to strong-arm tactics or guilting him into staying."

Brett squared his shoulders. "He'll want to stay if we own Geronimo. He has the best bloodline in Oklahoma *and* Texas. I've been trying to get these guys to invest in our horse-breeding program for months, and I've got them on the hook."

"The Lucky C doesn't need outside investors. We've done quite well on our own and don't need city boys poking their noses in our business."

Brett met Jack's gaze with a stubborn frown. "We do if you're unwilling to front the cash from the ranch funds to buy Geronimo."

"We're not buying Geronimo or any other studs." Jack leaned close to his brother and kept his volume low but his voice unflinching. "And we're not shifting any resources to raising cutting horses, saddle broncs, race horses or any other wild scheme you've got up your sleeve. Period. I'm the manager of this ranch, and I decide how and where to spend money. Cattle have gotten us where we are today, and they'll continue to be our business as long as I'm in charge. I see no good reason to change direction and risk everything Big J built."

Brett shook his head, clearly frustrated. "Damn it, Jack. I know what I'm doing! Daniel knows his business, and he'll take his business somewhere else if we don't make some changes around here."

Jack scoffed. "What did Daniel say when you proposed all this to him?"

Brett flinched. "I...haven't yet. I wanted to secure the deal before—"

Jack cut him off with a grunt and a head shake. "You

wanted more ammunition to lure Daniel to stay here. But he needs the freedom to decide his life without manipulation or bribes or guilt."

"I have his best interests—the *ranch's* best interests—in mind."

Jack rubbed his eyes with the pads of his fingers before speaking again. "And you're sure the two are one and the same?"

Brett looked confused. "Why wouldn't they be?"

Why, indeed. Except that Jack had often wondered what he'd missed by passing up the chance to strike out on his own when he'd been younger. He'd let the pull of the family business, his role as the eldest son, lock him into a life running his father's empire. He didn't regret his choice, exactly, but sometimes he just felt...constrained.

"Look, Brett, leave the business decisions to me. Okay? Tell your city slickers thanks, but no thanks, and drop this horse-breeding nonsense. Got it? If Daniel wants to stay at the Lucky C, he will...for his own reasons." Jack clapped his brother on the shoulder as he stepped back.

"Jack..." Brett's hands fisted, and his face hardened with displeasure and frustration.

But Jack felt it was better he settle the issue now, no holds barred, than have Brett continue to bug him about it and string the city slickers along. With a nod to the men from Dallas, he stepped away to look for his son. Seth had had plenty of time to change clothes and return to the party.

"Jack Colton!" His sister's voice pulled him up short as he passed the patio doors to the living room. "How dare you!"

He groaned internally as he turned. Now what?

Beside Greta stood a certain caramel-haired china doll, her eyes red from crying. Before he could repeat his order for Laura's cousin to get off the ranch, his sister seized his arm and dragged him through the crowd in the living room to an isolated corner of the foyer. Tracy followed.

"I am ashamed of you, Jack Colton!" Greta said, releasing his arm and scowling darkly. "I just found Tracy at our front door, crying. She says that you ordered her off the property. I hope I heard her wrong, because I can't believe any brother of mine would be so rude and inhospitable. This is *my* engagement party, and you have no right to say who attends and who doesn't."

Jack dragged a hand over his mouth, tamping down the irritation building in his blood. "She's not here because of your party, Greta. Or did she forget to tell you that part?"

"Did you kick her out?" Greta asked pointedly. "Did you not understand that she is *family*?"

He braced his hands on his hips and dug deep for patience. First Brett wrangling to tie Daniel to the ranch, now Greta shoving this woman's connection to Laura down his throat. He loved his family, but sometimes…

"She's Laura's family. Not ours. And yes, I asked her to leave. We'd said all that needed to be said."

"As Laura's family, that makes her Seth's family. And that, then, makes her *our* family."

Jack groaned long and loud. He could see where this was going. "Greta, don't interfere—"

"I've invited her to stay." His sister lifted her chin in a way that said the matter was settled. Being the youngest sibling and the only girl, Greta had gotten her way more often than not growing up. He wouldn't call her spoiled—not exactly—but Big J doted on her, and she was clearly and unequivocally Abra's favorite.

Jack glanced at Tracy, who was studying her shoes

and gnawing her bottom lip. "She didn't come here because of your party. She came to cause trouble with Seth."

Now Tracy's head jerked up. "I did not! I told you the last thing I wanted was to hurt Seth. I just want to meet him, get to know him, spend some quality time with h—"

"And I said *no*." He straightened his spine and clenched his hands at his sides. "Hell, no. No way. Not in a million years."

"Jack!" Greta scolded.

"I'm not stupid," he continued, undeterred by his sister, feeling his blood pressure rise and pulse at his temples. "I know this is a ploy to weasel your way into his life and establish some thin case you can take to a judge, trying to get visitation or shared custody or money or—"

Tracy was shaking her head, her face pale. "You don't listen so well, do you, cowboy? I've told you I don't want custody or your money!"

"But you *do* want to fill my son's head with stories about his mother." Jack aimed an accusing finger at her. "Things that will only raise more questions and—"

"He has a right to the truth!"

Greta gave a shrill referee-like whistle. "Both of you, to your corners!"

Abra appeared in the foyer, her eyes shooting daggers at the trio. "What is going on out here? I have guests! Greta, *you* have guests! And it is almost time for the official announcement. Shouldn't you be freshening up and finding your fiancé and a glass of champagne about now?"

Their mother added a look that said the question was actually a command, and she wouldn't be disobeyed.

"I'll be right there, Mother." Greta faced Jack again. "I have to go now, but Tracy is not going anywhere. I've invited her to stay as my guest. Not just for the party, but for an extended visit. She can have one of the spare rooms here in the main house."

Jack stiffened, feeling as if he'd been kicked in the chest by a bull. "You did what? Greta!"

"I hope for your sake and your son's that you will change your tune about letting her spend time with Seth. He has a right to know the truth, a right to know his maternal family."

Jack turned to glower at the blonde, whose expression had brightened. A pink blush tinted her cheeks, and her dewy blue eyes watched him with a light of expectation and hope. The odd tangle of lust and protectiveness he'd felt toward her in the stable reemerged, sending a shot of heat to his core. Tracy was the first woman in years to turn his head and stir this carnal reaction in him. And she'd be staying at the main house, just a short ride from the old ranch house where he lived with Seth. A cool drink in the midst of a ranch full of hot, thirsty brothers and hired hands. He didn't like the idea of that one bit, nor the flair of possessive jealousy that tickled his gut.

Tightening his jaw, he tore his gaze away, pushing aside the niggling desire.

She might look like an innocent china doll, but he feared she'd prove to be the Bride of Chucky.

He searched for an out and offered, "What is she supposed to do for clothes? I don't see a suitcase."

"She can borrow some of mine," Greta returned.

"Actually…I have a suitcase in my car. I'd planned to stay at a motel in town during my stay in Oklahoma. But if the parking valet could bring my car around from—"

"You planned to stay?" he asked, cutting her off.

She swallowed, then straightened her shoulders. "I hoped to have a few days to spend with Seth."

"See there? All settled." Greta nodded in satisfaction.

"You can…supervise her visits or…lay out parameters or something, if it makes you feel better." Greta waved a hand, clearly making up her suggestions off the cuff. "But since she'll be my guest, you *cannot* kick her off the ranch."

His sister smoothed the skirt of her sundress and stepped back. "Now, I have to go announce my engagement." She added a smile that reflected a touch of nerves. "Make nice, you two."

As she sauntered away, Greta gave him a little gloating grin, as if she'd bested him.

Jack knew better. Greta could allow Laura's cousin to stay in the main house, but he'd see to it Tracy got nowhere near Seth. His son was his whole world, and he'd protect him at all costs.

Tracy stood by herself in the cool marble foyer for long seconds after Jack gave her a warning glare and stomped off to join the party. She'd expected to have to sway Seth's father to her idea, but she'd never imagined he'd be quite so hostile and suspicious of her.

Laura had said there was no love lost between them after the divorce. Jack took his wife's leaving personally, she'd said. Understandable. Broken relationships had a way of being personal. But the wall Jack had erected to keep any hint of Laura or her memory out of his son's life was overkill in Tracy's estimation. She had her work cut out for her, breaking down his defenses and earning his trust.

Her head was telling her to run. Far and fast. She didn't need any part of another overbearing alpha male just months after freeing herself from Cliff. But her heart was telling her Jack Colton's bark wasn't a reflection of the soul inside. Laura had said Jack was a loving man, a softhearted father and a protective husband before things had gone south for them. Protective, Tracy could certainly believe, and she chose to believe that the rest lay beneath the hard surface she'd seen today.

The lean and sexy surface. She fanned herself, despite having long ago cooled off in the frigid AC after their hike to the stable. The heat that swamped her now came from deep inside. A purely female reaction to shaggy dark brown hair, broad shoulders and green eyes that glittered with passion when their owner got riled.

A rustling noise in the hallway to her right drew Tracy's attention, and she craned her neck to see what had caused the disturbance. She saw nothing at first, but when a side table with a large vase moved, rocking the vessel of flowers, she caught a glimpse of the boy who was the spitting image of Jack. "Seth?"

She stepped in that direction, sending the boy scurrying from his hiding place, jostling the side table again. The vase tipped forward, and Tracy rushed to catch it a split second before the crystal urn would have crashed to the floor. "Whoa! That was close."

She smiled at the boy as she righted the vase on the table. "I can't imagine your grandma would be too happy if that broke."

He shook his head, wide-eyed. "I'd have got a whuppin' for sure."

"Your father spanks you?" Tracy frowned, bothered by the notion.

He shook his head again. "Not Daddy. But Pa Pa might've, since it's Grandmother's flower thing. Daddy says he used to get whuppin's when he was bad."

She was relieved to hear Jack didn't spank his son, but tucked away the notion that Big J Colton had used corporal punishment on his. Discipline was one thing, but being all too familiar with domestic violence, Tracy worried where Big J might have drawn the line when spanking his grandson.

She made a mental note to investigate this further. If Seth was in any danger of harm, she'd do what it took to get him away from the Lucky C. For now she focused on the boy, her nephew, and gave him a friendly smile. "So you're Seth, huh?"

He nodded. "Yeah." Scrunching his nose, he corrected, "I mean, yes, ma'am."

Tracy chuckled. "A polite young man. That's nice."

"Daddy says 'specting elders is important." Seth rubbed his hand on his nose.

Tracy winced internally at being classified as an "elder." With a wry half grin, she said, "Manners are a good habit. He's right."

Seth narrowed a wary look on her. "Greta said you knew my mom. That you're…my family?"

Tracy caught her breath. Crouching to his level, she offered him another gentle smile. "You heard, huh?"

His eyes got big. "I wasn't spyin'! Honest! I just… well, I…"

She dismissed his concern with a head shake. "It's okay, hon. Yes, I knew your mom. She was my cousin. That makes you my cousin, too."

His dark eyebrows rose. "Really?"

"I'm your cousin Tracy." She held out a hand to him in greeting, but instead of a handshake, he slanted her a lopsided grin, stepped shyly closer and gave her a bear hug. Tracy's heart somersaulted, then flooded with joy. She blinked back the sting of tears the boy's warm greeting brought to her eyes, and embraced him back. His small body was slim but strong, and he smelled faintly of sweat and the last traces of a fresh soapy scent from his morning bath. Like his father, Seth wore his hair fairly shaggy, and it curled a bit from moisture at his neck.

"Cousin Tracy?" Seth backed out of their hug and wrinkled his nose.

Her chest filled to bursting as she heard him address her with the familial tag. "Yes, sweetie?"

"Why was my daddy mad at you?"

Her gut twisted. Just like that she was walking on eggshells, not wanting to cause problems, and handling delicate questions with the boy. "Well, I don't know that he was so much mad as he was—"

"Yep, he was," Seth said, nodding in certainty. "That was his mad voice, and he was all stiff, with his hands tight like this." He demonstrated the way Jack had fisted his hands. "And his face was bumping like it does when he's mad."

She blinked. "Bumping?"

He pointed to his temple. "Right here. When Daddy gets mad, his head goes bump bump bump."

She twisted her mouth as she deciphered the kid speak and decided Jack must have a blood vessel at his temple pulse point that throbbed when he was angry. "I see. Well…we had disagreed about something earlier, but it's nothing you need to worry about. Okay?"

Seth skewed his lips in thought, then lifted a lean shoulder. "Okay."

From the next room, Tracy her the clink of a utensil on glass and Big J's booming voice calling for the attention of his guests.

"Sounds like it's time for Greta's big announcement. Want to go with me to watch?" She offered her hand to Seth, and he took it with a nod.

"It's just about her and Mr. Mark gettin' married. I already know that stuff, but I'll take you in there."

"Why, thank y—" Before she could finish, he was towing her toward the living room entrance. She stumbled a step or two as she rose too quickly from her crouch. Seth moved with a hurried, boy-like trot that had her hustling to keep up. When they reached the amassed guests in the living room, he wove his way among them, dragging Tracy by the hand and causing her to jostle through the crowd as he led her to the front of the assembly gathered around Greta, Mark and the senior Coltons. Embarrassed to have been so boldly brought to the front, Tracy tried to sidle to the right, away from Abra and Big J's line of sight, but Seth tugged her arm, drawing her back to the center.

"Abra and I were thrilled to welcome our darling Greta to the family twenty-six years ago," Big J said to the room, his glass raised.

Tracy hunched her shoulders, trying to duck lower and make herself less obvious. Could she squat next to Seth? When she tried to stoop, she bumped the lady behind her, who scowled.

"Sorry," she whispered.

"After having four rowdy boys, we treasured our first and only baby girl," Big J continued, beaming at Greta.

Tracy cast a glance around the circle of onlookers, hunting for Jack's rugged face. Her attention snagged on the cowboy who'd parked her car when she arrived. He stood in a corner, his arms crossed over his chest, with a crooked grin on his face as he watched the proceedings. But his amused expression faltered at Big J's last statement. He ducked his chin, casting his gaze to the ground. For just a moment his brow wrinkled, so quickly Tracy almost missed it. But she was sure she'd seen a look that could only be described as hurt or crestfallen flicker across the cowboy's handsome face. A moment later he gave his head a small shake and returned his attention to Big J. Tracy couldn't help but feel a tug of sympathy for the man, without even knowing who he was or what had upset him.

"She's our pride and joy, and we are pleased to announce..."

Tracy's attention left the boisterous glee of the Colton patriarch, sensing rather than seeing Jack's hot stare from across the room. Her gaze darted to his, drawn like a magnet to his bright green eyes. A tingle like an electric shock skittered through her, speeding up her pulse. Her mouth dried, and she wished for one of the drinks the guests had hoisted in salute to the bride-and-groom-to-be. Not just because she stood out all the more for her lack of a glass for toasting, but because she could use something to wet her throat. Preferably something alcoholic, to help calm the flutter of nerves jangling in her core.

She was so entranced by Jack's level stare that when the crowd around her cheered and clapped, she gave a startled jolt. Pulling her hand free of Seth's, she joined the applause. Her appearance at the party with the boy had no doubt added to Jack's consternation. If making peace with Jack in order to gain access to Seth was her goal, she wasn't off to a good start. That needed to change. One way or another, she had to get past Jack's defensiveness, break down his walls and prove to him he could trust her with his son.

As the party ended and the last guests and media crew were sent away with hospitable smiles, Greta found Tracy out by the pool. Tracy had been watching Seth goof around on the grassy lawn with the cowboy who'd been her parking valet.

"Ready to go up and see your room?" Greta asked.

"Sure. Thanks." Tracy stood and smoothed the seat of her slacks, giving Seth and the handsome cowboy a last look. Remembering the expression of sharp disappointment that had crossed the man's face at the engagement announcement, she aimed her thumb over her shoulder as she followed Greta inside. "Who is that roughhousing with Seth?"

Greta glanced to the lawn. "Oh, that's Daniel. Another uncle."

Tracy frowned. "I thought you only had four brothers."

"He's a half brother." She sighed and lowered her voice to a wry, conspiratorial whisper. "The product of an 'indiscretion' on my father's part early in my parents' marriage." As she led Tracy through the living room Greta straightened an iron sculpture that had been knocked askew during the party. "When his mother died, Daniel came to live on the ranch." She raised her eyebrows and angled her head. "Much to my mother's chagrin. But my brothers and I count him as a full sibling and love having him here." She sighed and shook her head. "Mother still won't accept him, though."

"That explains the look, I guess," Tracy muttered to herself.

Greta's clattering footsteps on the marble foyer slowed. "I'm sorry? What look?"

Heat flushed Tracy's cheeks. She didn't need to be poking her nose in private family issues and stirring up problems while at the Lucky C. Her goal was to win favor and get to know her nephew, not be the conscience of the Colton clan.

"Oh, nothing." She forced a smile.

But Greta stopped walking and faced her, arching a well-manicured eyebrow. "Fess up. What do you know?"

Heaving a defeated sigh, Tracy wet her lips. "It's just

that…during your father's speech…when he was announcing your engagement…"

Her hostess's forehead dented with apprehension. "Go on."

"Well…" Tracy shifted her weight from one foot to another, feeling like a grade school tattletale. "I saw a look cross his face when your father was talking about having four sons before you were born. Daniel looked…hurt."

Greta closed her eyes slowly and grimaced.

"It was fleeting, and I could have imagined it, but…"

"Big J did say *four* sons, didn't he? I didn't even catch it at the time, or I'd have said something." Greta huffed in frustration. "No doubt he left Daniel out to appease Abra, but…poor Daniel. He denies to our faces that it still bothers him, but this kind of thing is bound to make him feel like an outsider. *Damn it.*" She grumbled the last under her breath as she resumed walking toward the wide stairs to the upper floors. "Thanks for telling me. I'll apologize to Daniel later for—"

"Oh, I…I can't imagine he'd want his discomfiture pointed out. Or the fact that I noticed. I don't want to be a source of trouble or strife in the family."

Greta flicked a dismissive hand. "I'll leave your name out of it."

That was something, but Tracy thought about the icy look Jack had given her earlier at the announcement. "I have enough to deal with earning Jack's trust. He really hated Laura a lot, didn't he?"

"Hated her? Heck, no. He loved her. More than he'll ever admit to any of us. You know how men bury that kind of thing. I think what he puts out there as ill toward Laura is the manifestation of his deep wounds. Her unhappiness at the ranch disappointed him. Her leaving him and their baby crushed him. Her distance and disinterest in their son after she left angered him. Laura hurt him on many levels, and he's put up walls. But don't be fooled. He never hated her. I think he wishes he could hate her. It'd make it easier to get over her abandonment."

"So his hostility toward me is—"

"Fear, most likely." Greta led her into a large, plushly appointed bedroom with a massive king-size sleigh bed, dark walnut furnishings and a recessed ceiling, framed with elegant crown molding.

Tracy caught her breath, taking in the beautiful decor.

"He's fiercely protective of Seth," Greta continued, apparently unaware of Tracy's momentary rapture. "That boy is everything to him. The idea that you could want to take Seth or disillusion—"

"But I don't!" Tracy countered quickly, snapping from her dazed admiration of the guest room.

Greta raised a hand. "I hear you. But Jack will be harder to convince."

Tracy's shoulders slumped. "Any advice where to start?"

Greta twisted her mouth in thought. "Action. You can talk until you are blue in the face and not convince him of anything. Jack is a doer. A man of action. If he sees you treating Seth with kindness and can witness evidence of your respect for his wishes regarding Seth, that will go further than any promises you make him. Laura made promises she didn't keep. You'll have to prove yourself to him before he'll listen to anything you say."

Chapter 4

That evening, Jack and Seth walked up to the main house to join Jack's parents, sister, Ryan and Brett for a family dinner. When she'd called him about coming to dinner, Greta had informed him that Eric, a trauma surgeon in Tulsa, had planned to be there, but had been called to the hospital. Mark had returned to town on business, and Daniel had begged off, claiming he had other mysterious plans.

Jack had had his fill of socializing for the day, even with his own family, and had been looking forward to a quiet evening with Seth. But his son had overheard the phone call and had bounced on his toes, begging to go. What could he say? Seth loved dinner at the main house, stuffing himself on the home-style foods Maria Sanchez, Abra and Big J's cook, prepared, and teasing with his uncles and aunt. The family connections were good for Seth, and the balanced meal was a far cry from the Tater Tots and hot dogs Jack had planned to make.

So here he was, heading back up to his parents' house with his son chattering animatedly beside him about the snake he'd seen out in the pasture that afternoon.

"Daniel said it wasn't the bad kind." Seth tugged the heavy back door open, his little-boy muscles straining. Jack no longer helped Seth with doors or his shoelaces or buckling his saddle straps—though he did double-check those before he let Seth ride. His boy was old enough to do things for himself and was determined to be self-sufficient. Jack encouraged him to learn ranch chores and be independent but caught himself wondering now and then where his baby boy had gone. Seth was growing up so fast.

"Some snakes are good, 'cause they eat the mice that get in the barn," he continued as they strolled through the mudroom and into the family room. "He says Sleekie can't catch all the critters, so we need some snakes around."

"Snakes?" Abra said as they joined the family. Jack's mother shuddered visibly and turned to speak to the woman next to her. "Vile creatures. Another reason I prefer to stay at the house and avoid the pens."

"I'm no fan of snakes myself," the woman agreed affably.

Jack recognized the voice and whipped his head toward the female guest. Tracy McCain. His gut rolled. He'd forgotten she was still here. Hadn't considered that she'd be at the family dinner. He slanted an irritated glance at his sister, and Greta's returned gaze was triumphant. "Jack, you remember Tracy, right?"

He clenched his back teeth, tightening his jaw and shoving down the growl of frustration that rose in his throat. "Yeah. I remember her." He cast a dark look at their guest that let her know exactly how he felt about her interloping.

"Hi, Tracy!" Seth chirped, peeling away from his father's side and skipping over to greet Laura's cousin.

Laura's cousin, therefore Seth's cousin. Hadn't Jack just thought that family connections were good for Seth? But Tracy's presence filled him with a sense of foreboding and unease that burrowed deep into his bones. Something about her left him off balance, made his skin feel hot and prickly, as if he'd been out in the sun too long. And the way her pale blue eyes watched him with that fragile, wistful expression fired unwelcome feelings of protectiveness in him. Protectiveness and—he gritted his teeth harder—lust. Yes, damn it. The woman's ethereal beauty and delicate femininity drew him in and riled his libido like crazy, a complication he didn't need if he was going to protect his son from her hidden agenda.

He'd opened his mouth to call Seth back to his side when his son opened his arms and fell against Tracy to give her a hug.

"Hi, sweetie," she answered with a warm smile as she returned the embrace. "Good to see you again."

Jack's heartbeat stumbled at Seth's trusting and loving gesture. Not for the first time, Jack wondered what his son was missing, not having a mother in his life. Abra loved her grandson, but had never been the warm, fuzzy type, even with her own children. Greta spoiled Seth when she was around, but she was such a tomboy, Jack didn't count her as a mother figure.

Seth, ever the gregarious soul, beamed up at Tracy and asked, "Do you want to see my pony after supper? His name is Pooh Bear, and he's all mine!"

"Pooh Bear? What a wonderful name. It reminds me of the Winnie the Pooh I had when I was little."

Seth brightened. "Me, too! That's why I named him Pooh!"

"Well, what do you know?" Tracy flashed a grin and combed her fingers through Seth's wild mane of hair. Seth leaned contentedly into the caress, and Jack could almost imagine him purring like a kitten.

His son always got his hair cut when Jack did, but in recent weeks, Jack had been too busy with the herd and calving to bother with a haircut. He dragged a hand through his own shaggy mop and tried not to imagine how it would feel to have Tracy's fingers tangling in his hair or stroking his skin. But his scalp tingled, anyway, with ghost sensations.

"My grandson is well on his way to being a fine horseman and cowboy, Miss McCain," Big J said, and flashed a smile that lacked the spark and full-wattage flirtation that was usually part of the old man's arsenal. Jack gave his father a considering glance and saw other evidence of fatigue. His shoulders were a bit more stooped, his face more lined and his cowboy's tan seemed a tad washed out. The engagement party had been a massive undertaking, but Jack was surprised by Big J's apparent post-party fatigue. His father was widely known to be an unstoppable force of nature. Bigger than life and always the last man standing.

Jack's puzzling over Big J's demeanor was sidetracked when Brett strode into the family room rubbing his belly. "Hey, y'all, when do we eat? I'm famished."

"After all you ate at the party? Where do you put it, you hog?" Greta gave her brother a playful jab.

"I can't help it. I'm a growing boy. Right, Seth?" Brett winked at his nephew, and Seth rolled his eyes.

"Well, now that we're all here, shall we go in?" Abra asked with a prim lift to her chin.

"Go in?" Jack muttered to Brett under his breath.

"Someone's been watching too much *Downton Abbey*," his brother returned quietly.

Jack arched an eyebrow. "And how would you know?"

Brett pulled a face. "I may have watched an episode or two with Greta. She monopolizes the TV in the family room on Sunday nights. The accents the women on that show have are kinda hot."

Jack gave his brother a slap on the back and a snort of laughter as he followed his mother, Greta and Tracy into the dining room.

Speaking of hot… The wispy sundress Tracy had changed into for dinner stopped above her knees and gave a tantalizing view of her slender legs and porcelain shoulders. Jack had the stray thought that Tracy would have to show extreme care with her skin if she went out on the ranch in the scorching June sun. She'd burn quickly and—

He shook his head. Tracy's skin and the relative risks of sun exposure for her were not his concern. If he had his way, she'd be long gone from the ranch before the question of sunburn could be an issue for her.

"Cousin Tracy, you can sit by me!" Seth said, patting the seat of the chair where Jack usually sat. His son blinked up at him. "Is that okay, Daddy?"

Jack paused, his hand on the back of the chair. "Oh… uh, sure." He pulled the seat out for her and helped her push up to the table before taking the only spot left, across the table from his son.

After Maria brought out their dinner, the family bowed their heads to say grace. When the prayer ended, Jack glanced across the table, and his gaze met Tracy's and held for a few lingering seconds. A pink flush filled her cheeks, and he felt his own body temperature rise.

Clearly, his libido recognized that Tracy McCain was an attractive woman. But his head wasn't ready to trust her.

"Tell us about yourself, Miss McCain," Big J said.

His father's voice broke the spell that had kept her staring back at Jack for long seconds. She jerked her attention to the end of the table as Big J passed a tray of roasted chicken and vegetables to her. Jack noticed that his father's hand shook a bit, adding to his earlier impression that Big J seemed uncharacteristically worn out this evening.

"I don't know that there's much to tell. I live in Denver, but I grew up outside of Colorado Springs and graduated from Colorado State with a degree in communications."

"Communications, huh?" Big J grunted. "And what are you doing with that degree?"

"Well, nothing at the moment. My husband didn't want me to work, and since his death, I haven't had much luck finding a job."

Jack paused with the serving spoon of wild rice hovering over his plate as his eyes lifted to Tracy again. She was unemployed? That lent credence to his theory that she was after money.

"You're a widow?" Greta asked, her tone soft and sympathetic. "I'm so sorry."

"What's a widow?" Seth asked, his mouth full of chicken.

"It means her husband passed away," Abra said quietly, when no one else spoke.

"Oh." Seth tucked into his dinner again, but Jack wasn't sure his son understood his grandmother's euphemism.

When Seth picked his chicken leg up with his hands

and took a big bite, Abra scowled. "You have a fork, Seth. Please use it."

"Oh, sorry." He gave her a chagrined look and earned another frown when he wiped his greasy hands on the cloth napkin.

"Can I help you cut your meat?" Tracy offered, reaching for his knife.

Jack opened his mouth to tell Tracy that Seth could cut his own meat, but Seth beamed up at her and nodded. "Sure. Thanks."

Where was his I-can-do-it-myself son? Seth had insisted on cutting his own meat since he was three years old. Jack watched, fascinated, as Tracy doted on him—helping serve him rice and peas, cut his meat and tuck his napkin in his lap—and Seth soaked up the coddling.

"How did your husband die?" Greta asked.

"Greta!" Abra scolded in a hushed tone.

"If you don't mind my asking…" Jack's sister added.

Jack had impertinent questions of his own. He needed to know more about Tracy and her history, her family connections, if he was to be prepared to protect his son.

Tracy flashed Greta an awkward smile, obviously uneasy with the question. She stared at her plate a moment, idly rearranging her English peas before answering.

He recalled their conversation in the stable earlier today. *He was shanked the second night he was in jail…*

"Car accident," she said quietly.

Jack's pulse kicked at the lie. Or was what she'd told him in the stable the lie? Either way, he'd caught her in a deception and intended to confront her about it. Later. He didn't want Seth to be a witness to any story she might invent to weasel out of the snare she'd caught herself in.

"How awful. I'm so sorry." Greta, seated on their

guest's left side, placed a comforting hand on Tracy's wrist.

"Wait," Brett said, screwing his face in a frown of confusion. "Didn't Laura die in a car accident? And she was your cousin, right?"

Tracy turned her face toward Brett, and the color leaked from her cheeks. "Yes."

Jack kicked his brother under the table, and Brett cut a side glare back at him. Jack had told Seth his mother had died right after he was born, and Brett's thoughtless comment threatened to expose the white lie. Clearing his throat and sending his brother a meaningful look, Jack said, "But that was a long time ago. Let's not talk about that now, huh?"

Tracy sent him a curious frown. "Not that long ago. Six months. Wh—"

"So, Greta, have you had any luck breaking that new colt we bought at the auction last month?" Jack asked, eager to change the subject before Seth caught on. The fact that he'd nearly been caught in a lie of his own didn't escape Jack, even if he could justify the disinformation he'd told Seth as being in his son's best interests.

"Jack," Greta said through clenched teeth, her manicured eyebrows dipping low in disapproval. "You interrupted Tracy."

He waved a fork toward their guest. "Oh, sorry," he said, though his tone contradicted him. "You were saying?"

Tracy gave her head a shake. "Forget it." She seemed glad to have the topic diverted from her, and faced Greta. "You train horses?"

Greta arched one scolding eyebrow at Jack, but nodded to Tracy. "I do. I work with the more difficult animals on the ranch and recently started taking clients who want a kinder method of training. I use operant conditioning and positive reinforcement instead of punishment and have had great success with even the most spirited animals." A grin tugged her cheek. "That's how I met Mark. He was a client."

Tracy smiled politely. "How wonderful."

"Did you ever see the movie *The Horse Whisperer*, Miss McCain?" Abra asked.

Tracy nodded. "Beautiful cinematography."

"I agree. Well, our Greta does much the same thing Robert Redford did in the movie." Abra gave her daughter a formal smile. "The term *horse whisperer* is more of a colloquialism than an official term, but you get the idea. Yes?"

"Sure."

"Can you ride a horse, Miss Tracy?" Seth asked, tugging at her arm.

"Well, I rode a pony at a fair when I was a kid, and I went on a trail ride once in Rocky Mountain National Park with my family as a teenager, but I'm not sure that counts."

"It's something," Greta said.

At the same time, Brett chuckled. "Hardly."

Tracy divided a grin between the two for their differing opinions. "Anyway, I haven't been on a horse in probably ten years or more, so I guess my answer is no."

"Oh." Seth's face fell in disappointment.

A thoughtful look crossed Greta's face as she stabbed a bite of chicken. "Ya know…I could take you riding tomorrow before I go back to OKC. Teach you a bit about horsemanship. It'll be fun. I'll show you the lay of the land."

Seth perked up. "Can I go?"

"Sure!" Greta said, just as Jack shook his head.

"Seth, I don't…" He let his sentence trail off as all eyes turned to him with mixed degrees of curiosity, disagreement and disapproval.

"You don't—" Greta prompted him, then immediately finished for him "—have any good reason not to let him join us. I'll keep a close eye on him."

"I know you will. I just…" He scowled at his sister and cast a disgruntled glance toward Tracy. When he hesitated, looking for a way to effectively deny Tracy access to his son, Greta swooped in.

"All righty, then. Meet me at the stables tomorrow morning at seven. We'll go out before it gets too hot. Then come back up to the house for a big ranch-style breakfast." She shot Seth a querying look. "Think you can be up that early and meet us?"

Seth glanced to his father, wide-eyed. "Daddy, what time do we get up?"

The truth was Jack typically had Seth up before dawn to help with ranching chores, but he had a perverse notion to let his son sleep in tomorrow. "Pretty early, usually."

"Tell you what," Brett said, then took a bite of biscuit and continued with his mouth full, "I'll pick you up on my way to the pens and help you get Pooh saddled up."

"Thanks, Uncle Brett!"

Jack shot his younger brother a frown that said *Die!* Brett answered with an innocent and bemused look. Clearly, Jack was alone in his mission to keep his ex-wife's scheming family away from Seth.

Fine. If his family was going to pave the way for Tracy to spend time with Seth, then he'd make himself available to monitor her interactions with his son. He wasn't about to let a pretty face and sweet smile fool him. His son was his first priority, and he'd protect his boy from anyone who tried to threaten his happiness or the life Jack had with Seth.

After dinner ended and the family moved to the family room to enjoy a glass of wine or a cold beer, Jack pulled Tracy aside for a private word. Even in the shadows of the small alcove where they stood, her pale blue eyes held a bright gleam of innocence that contradicted the motives he suspected were behind her visit to the ranch. Jack found that incongruity almost as annoying as his body's reaction to her bright, penetrating gaze.

He allowed his hand to linger on her soft skin, telling himself his grasp on her arm was to keep her as his captive audience until he'd said his piece. But a small voice in his head argued that he enjoyed touching her, standing close to her and seeing her eyes widen with anticipation when he hovered over her a bit too much.

"Is something the matter?" she asked.

"We just need to establish some boundaries, get some facts straight if you want to spend any time around my son." He drilled her with a hard look, hoping to assert an air of authority, but holding her gaze sent a shaft of desire to his belly. Damn but she was delicate and beautiful. Captivating in a way that spoke to everything male in him.

"What sort of boundaries?"

"For starters…" He clenched his back teeth, desperately shoving the distracting thoughts down so he could deal with the threat she posed. Like the Trojan horse, she might seem desirable on the outside, but what lurked inside held the real danger. "You're not to spend any time alone with Seth. I have to supervise any activity you do with him."

She rolled her eyes, expressing her opinion of his dictate.

"I'm serious. If I get word of you going behind my back and seeing Seth on the sly, I'll personally escort you off this ranch and have a restraining order filed within the day."

Her brow puckered indignantly. "A restraining order? Don't you think that's a bit excessive? I've told you I have no intention of harming Seth in any way."

"And I've said the truth of that remains to be seen. There are more than a few ways you could hurt him."

She huffed in exasperation and tried to leave. Jack blocked her, hating the tingle that shot through him when his chest and hips collided with hers. She took a step back and trembled visibly, her gaze now downcast. "Do you mind? I'd like to pass."

"We're not done."

Her shoulders drooped, and she seemed to struggle for the fortitude to meet his eyes again.

"I told Seth his mother died shortly after he was born."

Her shoulders snapped back and fire leaped to her eyes. "So you said earlier today. But that's—"

"That's the story you need to stick to. Telling him anything else will only hurt him. It will lead to questions about where she's been, why she left, why—"

"Why you lied to him?" Tracy interjected, her expression self-righteous.

Jack stiffened, his hands fisting at his sides. "I was trying to protect him. I thought it would be easier on him to think his mother died than to know she'd abandoned him. That she willfully walked away from her husband and child and didn't look back."

"What are you talking about? Laura *tried* to have a relationship with her son!" Tracy pressed her mouth into a taut line of disgust. "She tried to reach out to him, but you prevented her attempts to come back for visits. You wouldn't let him come see her, either."

"She made her choice. When she left, she was dead to us."

"Dead to you, maybe, but you had no right to keep Seth from her!"

Anger pulsed through Jack's blood and pounded at his temples. "I had every right! I'm his father!"

"And she was his mother!"

"Not after she threw him away. She signed full custody over to me when she left, in exchange for a tidy settlement. Maybe you can't buy love, but she certainly got paid well when she abandoned Seth."

Tracy looked away, her expression wounded.

"She didn't tell you that, did she? How she accepted a payout in exchange for her promise not to interfere with Seth or try to make any claim to him later in his life. She *sold* her right to my son, his inheritance and this ranch." He paused, then nudged Tracy's collarbone with his index finger. "And by extension, any right *you* or the rest of your family might have."

"I'm not after money. I just want to have a relationship with Seth. Why can't you believe that?"

The quiver of emotion in her voice chipped at the wall he'd erected. He could almost believe she meant what she said. Except...

"I make a habit of not believing known liars."

She stiffened in umbrage and grated, "I'm not a liar."

"Oh? What really happened to your husband? Is he even dead? Because you did, in fact, lie earlier. Either at dinner or in the stable." She blanched, and Jack gave her a smug grin. "Yeah. I caught it. You told me this afternoon your husband was killed in prison, stabbed by another inmate."

Tracy's doll-like features crumpled, and she looked as if she might be ill. "He was. But I couldn't very well say that at dinner with Seth listening."

Jack folded his arms over his chest. "I see. So you plan to base this relationship you want with my son on lies? Can you see why I don't trust you?"

Her shoulders drew back defiantly, causing her small breasts to jut toward him. "I was trying to protect him from the ugliness of the truth! He's too young to hear about such things as prison murders and shanks made from a sharpened toothbrush."

"And when he first asked about his mother, he was too young to know about a mother who could walk away from her family for purely selfish reasons."

Tracy opened her mouth, clearly planning to defend her cousin.

"Don't even start," Jack said, stopping her by pressing a finger to her lips.

Tracy jolted as if his touch had caused a static shock, drawing a sharp breath and flinching.

Too late, he realized the mistake of his move. He, too, felt a crackle of something electric that briefly sidetracked his thoughts and caused a tremble deep in his marrow.

Their gazes clashed for a moment, and he withdrew his hand, rubbing his thumb over the spot in his finger that still tingled.

From the next room he heard Seth's youthful laugh as Brett roughhoused with his nephew, and Jack recalled the point he'd been making. "I was there, not you. I was the one she divorced, the one she argued her case to, the one left cleaning up in her wake. I was the one who paid her settlement and stayed up nights with a colicky baby after she walked out. I have every right to determine what my son knows about Laura and what remains unspoken. You *will not* tell him anything that contradicts what he now knows about his mother. Or you will be removed from the ranch and Seth's life if I have to carry you to the highway myself."

Tracy's gaze flitted to his arms and chest, as if imagining him making good on his threat. She swallowed hard, and her feet shuffled slightly as she shifted her weight. He could see the pulse point at the base of her throat fluttering, and he was swamped by a primitive urge to taste the skin there. To suckle her neck, nip the skin and feel that rhythmic pulsing with his lips.

Hellfire! What was he doing? He didn't need to be indulging in lustful fantasies about this woman if he was going to do his job as a father and protect Seth from her meddling.

Tracy took a step back from him and bumped the wall behind her. Flexing her hands and wiping her palms on the skirt of her dress, she wet her lips and raised her chin. "I won't tell Seth anything that contradicts you." The nervous glint in her liquid eyes belied the set of her shoulders. "But neither will I lie to him if he asks me directly."

Jack gritted his teeth. "Ms. McCain, I'm warning you…"

"You don't need to make threats, Jack. I told you I have Seth's best interests at heart, same as you." She placed a trembling hand on his arm and pushed at him. "Now let me pass."

He didn't move right away, stubbornly keeping her trapped to let her know he would have the final say, not only with Seth but in this discussion. Finally, he stepped aside and swept a hand toward the living room, granting her passage. She stalked away, leaving a hint of her sweet floral scent behind. He experienced an unwanted, but not unpleasant, visceral reaction to the heady honeysuckle aroma she trailed in her wake. Maybe, he thought wryly, the vixen had gotten the last word, after all.

Chapter 5

Early the next morning, Tracy hitched a ride with Brett in a utility vehicle across the wide ranch yard to the outbuildings. First stop, Jack's house to pick up Seth.

As Brett parked in front of the age-worn wood-and-hand-carved-stone house, Tracy admired the ranch-style home where Jack and Seth lived. Where Laura had once lived. How could this gorgeous abode and beautiful setting not have been enough for Laura?

"This used to be the main house, before Abra had the new house built," Brett said, tooting the tinny-sounding horn of the utility vehicle. "It's over a hundred years old, but has been kept in good repair through the years."

Seth came scampering through the front door with Jack close behind. He raced up to her like an eager puppy, grinning ear to ear. "Hi, Miss Tracy!"

"Good morning. Aren't you full of energy so early in the day?" She ruffled the boy's still-sleep-rumpled hair. "What's your secret?"

He gave her an I-don't-know shrug.

"Sugar," Brett said under his breath. "Jack lets the kid eat all the chocolate cereal he wants for breakfast."

"Wrong," Jack said as he drew close to them. "He only gets that crap when he stays at the main house."

Tracy shifted her attention to the older Colton brother, and her pulse did a little morning jig. Jack was obviously fresh from his shower, his hair still damp and curling near his collar. His work clothes were crisp and carried the clean scent of laundry detergent, and he had recently shaved his square jaw and angled cheekbones. Beneath the rim of a black cowboy hat, his eyes held an especially magnetic emerald gleam in the early-morning sun. His blue jeans hugged his lean hips and his muscled thighs in a way that left no secret that Jack was every bit as fit and toned as she imagined a career rancher and horseman would be.

Her mouth dried, and her palms sweated. Good-looking though he was, Brett hadn't had this gut-tightening effect on her when he'd appeared on the back porch, ready to escort her to the stable. Jack had a certain...*something* about him that spoke to her. An elusive additional quality that made her nerves spark and heightened her senses.

"Hop in, buddy. I have things to do," Brett told Seth, aiming a thumb at the back of the MULE.

When Seth started for the backseat of the utility vehicle, Jack caught the back of his shirt and pulled him up short. "Not needed. He can walk over with me. If Seth's going out for a ride on the property, I'm going, too."

Tracy sat taller, a tickle of apprehension in her gut. "You don't have to go. He'll be well cared for. Greta and I will keep a close eye on—"

"Ms. McCain, do you remember our conversation last night in the alcove?"

How could she forget? Cornered by his muscular body and lectured to as if she were a schoolgirl, she should have been frightened. His body language and demeanor had been similar to the intimidation techniques Cliff had used. But she'd sensed two things in Jack that had calmed her fears.

First, a well-controlled restraint. The passion behind Jack's intensity last night had been a love for his son, whereas Cliff's violent and malevolent rages had been rooted in a savage cruelty and lack of self-control.

And second, she'd felt a strong undercurrent of attraction. While she was unnerved by that sensual spark between them, she couldn't call it fear. She felt safe with Jack Colton, yet vulnerable to him because of her body's carnal response to his presence.

"I meant what I said about supervising your time with Seth," he continued. "We'll meet you there in five." His clipped tone left no room for argument.

Oo-kaay. So Jack would be joining them on the horseback excursion around the property. Her stomach fluttered a little with nervous energy. Novice that she was, she prayed she didn't embarrass herself in the saddle in front of Jack.

Greta had arrived at the stable ahead of them and greeted Tracy with a cheery hello. Brett waved goodbye and made a gesture with his hand to indicate she should phone him when she was ready to be driven back up to the main house, since the walk was two miles. Her feet ached from having made the trek yesterday in her "sensible" pumps, which had proved highly unsensible for a ranch. This morning she'd worn tennis shoes and jeans, the only jeans she'd brought with her. Tracy could see that a shopping trip for more practical ranch clothes would be on the agenda for that afternoon or tomorrow.

Her hostess had a dark brown horse with a black mane and tail already saddled and was leading a lighter brown horse out of the stable. "Hey there, Tracy! I've got Mabel all saddled and ready for you."

Tracy eyed the dark brown horse with a bit of trepidation. She'd never spent much time around horses, and she was unsure what to do with the mare. She wanted to exude more confidence than she felt, nonetheless, so she strode forward and reached for Mabel's nose.

"Wait!" Greta called. "Don't approach her from straight on. That's her blind spot. Come at her at an angle so she can see you. Then give her the back of your hand to smell, like when you greet a dog for the first time."

Tracy sucked in a deep breath and edged sideways, adjusting her approach. "Hi, Mabel," she said sweetly and held out her hand as she neared.

The mare snuffled and sniffed her, and when Mabel lowered her nose, Tracy patted her neck.

"That's the way," Greta said with a grin as she slung her saddle over her horse. "Mabel is a sweetheart. She's the horse we always give visitors, since she's so easygoing. Just be firm with her, or she'll want to dally in the fields to nibble all day."

The thud of footsteps drew Tracy's attention as Seth ran up and climbed on the rungs of the corral fence. "Are you gonna ride Mabel, Miss Tracy?"

"Seems so." She gave the mare another pat and glanced past Seth to his father. Once again a bolt of electric attraction streaked through her, stealing her breath. Jack was so ruggedly handsome, his stride so confident and relaxed…

"Let's go, buddy." Jack ruffled his son's hair as he passed. "Bring Pooh out of his stall, and let's get him saddled."

Seth hopped down from the fence and grabbed her hand. "Come on, Miss Tracy. You can help me."

"Oh…uh, Seth, I don't—" The rest of her protest was lost in a gasp as a black animal streaked from the shadows and ran right in front of her, nearly tripping her.

Seth laughed. "You're not scared of Sleekie, are you, Miss Tracy?"

She pressed a hand over her runaway heart and looked for the animal in question. A black cat sat on a hay bale in the corner of the stable, tail swishing. "Is that Sleekie? The cat?"

"Yep," Seth said, tugging her forward again. "Don't worry. Black cats aren't really bad luck. You don't have to be scared."

She smiled sheepishly. "I know. She just startled me is all."

"Her real name is Oh La La Sleek. But we just call her Sleek or Ohla, 'cause Daddy says her real name is a mouthful."

"I see." An amused grin twitched Tracy's lips as she listened to the little boy chatter. Pausing, she cast a backward glance to the end of the stable, where Jack paused to give Sleek a leisurely head scratch before taking a coiled rope off a hook on the wall. His gentle attention to the cat was evidence of what Laura had said about his tender side. *Tough as leather on the outside, but soft as whipped butter toward anyone he loves.* Tracy felt her heart melt like that same butter on a hot waffle.

"I can lead Pooh myself—" Seth called, interrupting her food analogy.

Maria Sanchez had been preparing breakfast as Tracy had left. The aromas of pork and warm maple syrup had made her stomach growl, and she could hardly wait to dig into the bacon and waffles waiting when they returned from their ride.

"—but Daddy has to check my saddle. He says that's just in case. He wants to be sure I'm safe." Seth opened the gate to a stall and walked in to greet his pony. "Morning, Pooh! Wanna go for a ride?"

Tracy approached Pooh from an angle, as Greta had instructed with Mabel, and held her hand out to the pony.

Seth clipped a lead onto the pony's bridle and tugged him forward. "Move it, Pooh!"

Tracy followed as the pony plodded out into the alley, and Jack helped his son ready the small horse for their ride. As Jack worked, Seth kept up his excited dialogue about being the ring bearer in Greta's wedding, the herd of cattle and his first loose tooth, one topic flowing into the next as if they were related. He opened his mouth to point out his wiggling incisor.

"Thee?" Seth lisped around the dirty finger, and Tracy tried not to think about the germs the boy would swallow as a result. Boys and dirt went together, she figured, craning her neck to admire the loose tooth.

"Wow! That's almost ready to come out!" she enthused, then glanced up as Greta strolled into the stable to check on them.

Seth bobbed his head. "I can't wait! Uncle Brett says if I put it under my pillow, the tooth fairy will bring me twenty dollars!"

Jack choked and coughed. He sent his son a wide-eyed look of dismay before pulling a face and returning to the buckles and straps he was adjusting.

Greta laughed and leaned close to her older brother. "Even the tooth fairy is subject to inflation."

"I think Brett's about to owe me money," he muttered

in return. Soon Jack had his saddle buckled and Seth's double-checked, and the group was ready to ride.

When it was her turn to mount up, Jack moved behind Tracy and wrapped his big hands around her waist, giving her a boost into the saddle.

"How much do you remember about riding?" he asked as she settled on Mabel's back.

"Not much. It's been ten years since that trail ride in the Rockies."

He grunted in acknowledgment and let his hand linger on her hip as he handed her the reins. "Leave a little slack in the reins, but not too much. Keep your head up and watch where you are going, not the horse," he said, but she was distracted by the heat of his palm on her hip. His handprint felt seared into her with a tantalizing tingle.

"Keep the ball of your foot in the stirrup. If you need help, don't panic or shout, you'll scare the horse. I'll be right behind you."

She gave a nod of understanding as he pulled Mabel's harness, and the mare followed Greta's horse and Seth's pony as they set out.

Tracy squeezed the leather straps in her hand as they headed across the nearest field. Seth whistled to the cows as if they were dogs and laughed as calves romped and ran to their mothers.

"As long as we're out here," Jack called, loud enough for his sister to hear, "we should use the time to check the fences up in the north pasture."

Greta signaled a thumbs-up and steered her horse toward a gate in the main field. Jack swung down from his saddle to open the gate and let them through before securing the fence and mounting Buck again in one smooth, practiced motion. His athleticism and natural agility prodded Tracy's pulse to a dizzy cadence. Jack personified every romantic cowboy she'd ever seen in movies or read about in novels. Lean, tough, handsome and so sexy.

"Tracy!" he shouted, yanking her guiltily out of her daydreaming. She'd been staring at Jack's snug jeans and the skillful way he managed his horse with subtle body movements and tongue clicks. He motioned for her to join the group, which was leaving her behind. "You have to pull up on her reins and make her obey your direction. Mabel will lollygag all day if you let her."

"Oh...right." Tracy drew and released a cleansing breath, then pulled hard on the reins and goaded her mare. "Time to go, Mabel. Come on, sweetie. Yah!" She tried giving the mare a light kick with her heels. Mabel only chewed another mouthful of prairie grass.

"Let her know you're boss," Greta called. "Pull harder on the reins. Bring her head up."

Tracy tried again, afraid to hurt the horse by tugging too hard. She certainly didn't want to anger the thousand-plus-pound beast she was sitting on.

Jack rode back to her and reached for her reins. "Come on, Mabel." He brought the horse's head up and gave the mare a slap on the rump to get her moving.

Mabel trotted forward, bouncing Tracy in the saddle. After a few minutes, they reached the northern pasture and rode along the fence line so Greta and Jack could survey the condition of the barrier.

"So, uh, what's the goal here?" Tracy asked.

"Maintenance," Jack said, pulling alongside her.

"If ya see a post that's broke, holler," Seth said matter-of-factly, as if he were ranch manager instead of his father.

"Fences are always getting knocked down or damaged

by weather or by…" Greta glanced to Seth and cleared her throat before finishing. "Umm…amorous bulls."

Tracy chuckled. "Pardon?"

"If there is a cow in heat in a neighboring field," Jack explained, "a bull might knock down a fence trying to get to her."

He gave Tracy a level look, and she felt the rising tingle in her cheeks as she flushed. "Oh."

"Generally, we manage the breeding program, which includes keeping the cows and bulls in separate pastures. But every now and then, a bull gets out of containment. The instinct to breed is a powerful thing, and pasture fence won't hold a one-ton bull answering that most primitive impulse."

Jack's gaze lingered, a sensual heat filling his piecing stare. Tracy shifted restlessly on her saddle, her skin suddenly feeling both too tight and prickly, as if sunburned.

"There's one, Daddy!" Seth called, heading off with his pony at a canter.

Tracy jerked her attention away from Jack's weighty gaze to see what Seth had found. By squinting against the morning sun, she spotted a leaning fence post some distance off. "How did he see that?" she muttered.

"The boy's got eagle eyes. Better than his ole dad's," Jack said, before riding ahead to join his son.

Before Tracy could reach them, Seth was already off Pooh and messing with the broken post. While Jack opened a flap on his saddlebag and brought out a few tools, his son pushed on the wooden post and flapped the loose barbed wire. Greta reined her horse next to Tracy and swung down with an easy finesse to help. Tracy gripped the saddle horn and eyed the distance to the ground with trepidation.

Here goes nothing… She stood in her stirrups and

swung her foot over Mabel's back, only to have her already tired muscles wobble as she tried to hop smoothly to the ground. Instead she stumbled awkwardly, nearly landing on her butt. When she regained her balance, she shot a rueful glance toward Jack and found him watching her with an amused grin twitching one cheek.

"Just call me Grace," she said with a good-natured eye roll, earning a wider smile from Jack. The rare smile transformed his face from ruggedly handsome to breathtaking, and Tracy did, in fact, struggle to draw air into her suddenly tight lungs.

A cry from Seth shattered the moment, and both Jack and Tracy whirled toward the boy, who held out his bleeding hand with tears filling his eyes.

She rushed forward, concerned about him, as Jack knelt to examine the injury.

"What happened?" Greta asked, peering over her brother's shoulder.

"I hurt my hand on a poker on the wire. It's bleeding lots!" Seth gaped at his injury with childlike horror.

Jack used his shirttail to wipe the blood from Seth's hand and judge the extent of the wound. "Aw, it's not so bad. Barely a scratch. We'll slap a Band-Aid on there, and you'll be good to go."

When his father rose to retrieve some first-aid supplies from his saddlebag, Seth turned to Tracy with puppy-dog eyes set to full power and his chin quivering. "It really hurts."

Sympathy arrowed through her and, crouching, she held out her arms. Seth fell immediately into her embrace, and she examined his hand herself. "You poor thing. I bet that's sore. Don't worry, we'll make it all better."

Seth snuggled close. "Will you kiss it? Dillon says his mommy kisses his boo-boos."

"Of course I will, sweetie." And she did, giving the palm of his hand a big smacking kiss, plus another on his forehead.

Seth smiled through his sniffles and leaned his head on her shoulder. "Thanks, Miss Tracy."

Jack glanced back at his son and frowned. "Seth, it's not that bad. You've had worse and didn't cry this much over it. Don't be a baby."

Tracy glared at Jack. "He's not a baby, but even big boys need a little TLC from time to time."

Jack pulled a disgruntled face as he brought disinfectant spray, a sterile wipe and a Band-Aid over and knelt in front of them. "Okay, Spud. Let me see it."

"Can Tracy do it?" he asked in a timid voice.

Jack blinked, looking a tad hurt. "Well, I guess."

She sent him a silent apology with her eyes as she accepted the wound-cleansing spray and wipe from him. Holding Seth's hand gently in position, she poised the antibiotic spray. "Okay, close your eyes and think about your favorite video game."

Jack scoffed.

Ignoring Jack, she asked, "Ready?"

Seth bobbed his head and wrinkled his nose in dread.

Tracy spritzed the puncture wound with disinfectant, and Seth whimpered.

"Are you thinking about your favorite game?" Tracy asked and blew gently on the wound.

"Yeah, but it stings."

"I know, sweetie, but you're being very brave."

Jack grunted again, and Tracy elbowed him, shooting him a quelling look.

With a shake of his head and a frown of discontent,

Jack rose and walked away, turning his attention to the fence post that needed to be pounded back in place.

She continued doting on the little boy, savoring the opportunity to mother him, while Jack and Greta replaced the post and tightened the barbed wire.

For her efforts, Seth gave Tracy a kiss on the cheek. The sweet gesture burrowed deep in her heart and stirred an ache for children of her own to cuddle and nurture. As she rose from the ground, her muscles protesting with a stiff throb, she sensed Jack's gaze on her.

A side glance confirmed as much, and rather than avoid him and his reproach, she marched over to him and raised her chin. "I'm sorry if I overstepped, but little boys need motherly coddling every now and then."

Jack raised an eyebrow, clearly skeptical. "He was playing you. He knew you'd fuss over him, so he pulled out the crocodile tears and theatrics for your benefit."

"It may have been an act, but have you considered that maybe he did it because he misses having a mother to dote on him?"

Jack narrowed his eyes and braced a hand on his hip as he faced her. "Are you implying I don't give my son enough attention?"

"Not at all. By all indications, you've been a great father." Her assessment seemed to appease him a bit. "But there's a reason children have a mother and a father. Mothers provide something fathers can't."

Turning back to his saddlebag, where he stowed his tools, he shook his head. "Bull. I'm doing just fine caring for my son alone."

"I'm not criticizing. Single parents raise healthy, well-adjusted children all the time. I don't mean to imply otherwise. I'm just saying a little boy needs what a mother can—"

"Daddy!" Seth called from the back of his pony, interrupting her. "Can I ride ahead with Aunt Greta?"

Jack jerked a nod. "Sure, go on."

The little boy spurred his pony and set off.

When Tracy opened her mouth to continue making her case, Jack cut her off, waving a finger toward Mabel. "Need a hand up?"

Taking her cue that the subject of Seth's need for mothering was closed, she eyed the large horse and grimaced. "I, um…"

He strode over to Mabel and held the stirrup steady. "Come on."

When Tracy fixed her foot in it and pushed off the ground, he planted his hand on her bottom and gave her a needed boost to propel her into the saddle. She gasped at the intimacy of his touch, and desire like Fourth of July sparklers crackled in her veins. Even after he'd sauntered back to Buck and climbed into his own saddle, Tracy could feel the heat of his hand on her buttock, as if he'd branded her. Jack hung back, waiting for her to ride ahead, and she tugged hard on Mabel's reins, bringing her head up from her continued snacking.

"You should consider getting Seth a tetanus shot." Her voice croaked, giving away her lingering jitters as Mabel strolled past Buck and they moved on down the fence line. Tracy sat taller in her saddle, pretending confidence she didn't feel around Jack. Her attraction to him rattled her and undermined her mission to build a relationship with Seth. "Despite your dismissal, that was a pretty deep puncture wound."

"He's had one." Jack paused, then added, "But… thanks." A moment later, he cleared his throat and added, "I appreciate your concern. And your tending to him."

The wind blew a wisp of her hair in her face, and she

tucked it behind her ear as she gave Jack a nod. "My pleasure. He's a wonderful little boy."

A grin ghosted across Jack's lips in acknowledgment, and he fell silent for a moment. His expression grew pensive, then a pained look crossed his face. "He's my life. I'd be lost without him." Jack sighed and cast a side glance her way. "I guess that's why I get so…protective of him. Overprotective, if I feel a threat to him."

"And you see me as a threat?"

He didn't answer right away. Finally, he muttered, "I did."

His use of the past tense startled her. "And now?"

"I believe you don't want to hurt him." Jack's concession on that point was a major victory in her eyes. But then he added, "However…threats come in many forms. What if he grows attached to you and then you go home and…"

He let his sentence trail off, and she recognized a wounded look in his eyes she knew he would never vocalize. One of disappointment and inner pain.

Greta claimed Jack had loved Laura. Had her cousin broken his heart when she'd left? Was the source of his anger and resentment a lingering ache from lost love? Maybe part of Jack's protectiveness for his son was rooted in his own defensive walls. Was he afraid to let a woman back in his life—and therefore his son's—because he had never recovered from the wounds of his broken marriage?

"Miss Tracy!"

She shifted her attention to Seth, who was riding back to them with a fistful of wildflowers. "Whatcha got there, sweetie?"

"Flowers. They're for you." He rode up beside her and handed the scraggly bouquet to her.

Holding the horn of her saddle so she wouldn't fall, she reached down to take the yellow and purple blossoms. "Why, Seth! These are lovely. Thank you."

She took a big sniff for show, though they didn't seem to have any discernible fragrance.

Seth beamed. "Aunt Greta says girls love getting flowers."

"She's right. The best part for me is knowing these are from you."

Clearly pleased with himself, Seth tugged Pooh's reins, turned the pony and rode off again.

When Tracy glanced at Jack, she saw the wrinkle of concern in his brow, and she lifted her chin. "Jack, this doesn't have to end badly. If you'll let me, I could have an ongoing relationship with Seth. I don't want to disappear from his life. I want to know him. Watch him grow up. Be a part of his life in a way Laura never could."

Jack's square jaw tightened, making his countenance appear all the more rough-hewed and severe. "We'll see. One step at a time."

His bright green eyes mirrored the intensity of his voice, and she felt an answering tremor deep in her core. Not of fear, but of yearning. A delicious, tantalizing stirring that made her heart beat faster, her nerves tingle and her breath quake. Jack Colton spoke to the very root of her. Her soul. Her marrow. Her heart.

When planning her mission here to meet Seth, she'd never considered the possibility of falling for Seth's father. But now she needed to examine how that might change things. Because she could feel herself succumbing to Jack Colton's spell.

Tracy had certainly cast her spell over Seth. Jack brought up the rear of their little parade and kept a close eye on the interaction between his son and Laura's cousin. Their conversation was superficial and lighthearted, eliciting frequent laughter from both. His son's giggles never failed to lift his own spirits, the sound so full of youthful glee. And Tracy's laugh had its own mesmerizing effect on him. At first, her chuckling sounded rusty, as if she had to dust it off from infrequent use. That fit the image he'd built of her, his suspicion that she'd come from an unhappy, abusive marriage. As the ride progressed and she relaxed with Seth, her laughter loosened up, the musical notes tickling Jack's gut like bubbles in champagne.

He noticed, too, the comfortable way she sat her horse. For someone who'd been in a saddle only once or twice before, she had a natural grace and skill. And if he found himself staring at the curve of her bottom and the way her slim legs hugged Mabel's flanks, it was because he was admiring her horsemanship and not the way her jeans fit her trim build. *Yeah, right, Colton. Who do you think you're kidding?*

He blew out a sigh, tamping down the kick of lust that coiled like a rattlesnake in his core. After ten years of a reckless, wild lifestyle, followed by a short marriage, he'd been virtually celibate for the past five years. His choice. He'd wanted to focus all his energy and attention on Seth, and making the ranch prosper during tough economic times. But the sexual drought had left him all the more primed and tuned to chemistry he sensed with Tracy—or that's what he told himself. Admitting he had a natural rapport and physical connection to Laura's cousin left him edgy and off balance.

"Jack, do you see this?" Greta called from the front of their group. The uneasy tone of her voice as much as her question brought him out of his reverie.

He followed her pointing finger to the old family cemetery, situated under the branches of a large, sprawling oak tree, where Big J's ancestors had been buried. Jack didn't see what had disturbed Greta right away, but when he looked closer, squinting against the bright sun, he saw the small pile of dirt and the shovel that lay next to a hole in the ground. Was there a grave robber loose on the Lucky C?

"What is it, Daddy?" Seth asked, standing in his stirrups to see across the meadow.

"I don't know." Jack tugged Buck's reins and headed toward the cemetery. "Seth, wait here with Tracy while I take a closer look."

"Why can't I come?" Seth whined, but Jack didn't linger to debate his order. Greta fell in behind him, and they dismounted together at the edge of the low fence that surrounded the small family graveyard.

Jack walked first to the pile of dirt and lifted the shovel that had been left there. He recognized it as one used in the stable for mucking out stalls.

Greta rounded the small pile of dirt and peered into the hole that had been dug. "It's not one of the marked graves, but—" She stopped abruptly, gasping and stumbling back from the freshly dug pit.

"Greta?" Jack hurried to his sister. "Are you all right?"

She aimed a shaky finger toward the hole. "I'm better than whoever that is." When he frowned in question, she pointed again. "Look."

Even before he peered down into the earth, apprehension tightened his gut. At the bottom of the freshly dug hole lay the pale bones of a tiny human skeleton.

"It's a baby, isn't it?" Greta asked, her voice choked with tears.

Jack clenched his back teeth so hard his jaw ached. "Seems to be, judging from the size."

"Who is it?" she asked, her voice trembling. "Or maybe I should ask *whose* is it, considering there's no headstone."

"Good question." He swiped a hand over his face and stepped back from the grave. He had no way of guessing how old the bones might be or how long they'd been buried.

Greta edged closer to him and rested a hand on his forearm. "What do you think happened to it? Did Big J ever mention to you about a baby being buried here?"

Jack shook his head. "Not that I remember. If it was a relative of Big J's, why isn't there a headstone?"

"I don't like this, Jack." Greta's voice cracked, and her breathing was shallow. "It doesn't feel right. And I don't just mean because a baby died. Why would someone dig up the bones? Why would they leave the grave open like this? Just…abandoned and exposed?"

"It's not right." He turned slowly, surveying the area for further clues about what had happened and who'd been there. "It's not right at all."

"What is it, Dad?" Seth's voice called from the bottom of the hill.

"Stay put!" Jack shouted back. He didn't need his son having nightmares about dead babies and open graves. Bad enough the sight was burned into his own brain and Greta's.

"What do we do?" his sister asked, her fingers tightening on his arm.

"We do nothing. Treat it like a crime scene, and don't touch anything." He pulled out his cell phone and checked for signal strength. As with many of the more remote spots on the ranch, he had no reception here. He put his arm around his sister's shoulders and guided her toward the horses. "When I get back to the house, I'll call

Ryan. If there's no official record of the baby's burial, I'm guessing the coroner will have to exhume the remains."

Greta cast another worried glance over her shoulder to the cemetery before mounting her horse. "What good will that do?"

"They may be able to tell us how long ago the baby died, and if it died from foul play. A DNA profile could tell us more about who the baby is."

Greta gave a visible shudder before snapping her reins and heading back down the hill. "It's so creepy…and sad. That poor baby!"

"There could be a simple explanation," Jack said, trying to reassure his sister, though the image of the tiny skeleton still haunted him, as well. "Remember, infant mortality was much higher even as recently as fifty years ago."

"What was it?" Seth asked again as they approached.

"Nothing for you to worry about. Let's head back to the house. We all have work to do."

Tracy rode up close to Jack as Greta turned for the stable with Seth leading the way.

"Well?" she asked in a quiet tone.

He hesitated, casting a grim glance at her. "Someone dug up an unmarked grave, exposing the skeleton of a baby."

Tracy's hand flew to her mouth. "Oh, dear Lord! Who—what—?"

"Yeah. My sentiments exactly."

"Oh, Jack…" Beneath the hint of sunburn that colored her cheeks, Tracy's face was as white as a ghost. Her blue eyes grew wide and looked haunted. A knot of regret twisted inside him for the lost joviality she and Seth had shared earlier. Jack already missed the bubbly sound of her laughter and the light of her teasing smile.

He put away the reasons for his powerful reaction to her, to examine later. Right now they had the upsetting find at the cemetery to deal with and a ranch to run. His unexplained attraction to Tracy would wait for another day.

Chapter 6

Half an hour later, they returned to the stable, and though stiff and a bit sore, Tracy had to admit she'd found the horseback ride exhilarating—save for the gruesome discovery at the cemetery.

When she said as much, Greta offered to give her an official riding lesson. It would help reduce her aches by training her to stand in the stirrups instead of bouncing in the saddle.

"I'd love that. Thanks." Tracy watched from the corner of her eye as Jack led his horse and hers into the stable and started removing the saddles and blankets.

"I have wedding-related appointments this week in Oklahoma City, but..." Greta pinched the bridge of her nose and shook her head, clearly still rattled by her sad find. "Um...I'll be back Thursday afternoon. So maybe that evening?"

Tracy followed Greta into the shade of the stable and

blinked as her eyes adjusted to the dimmer light. "Sure. It's a date."

Seth was already sponging Pooh off, cooling the pony down. Tracy watched him for a moment, amazed at what he could do at age five. If Seth could tend Pooh, she needed to learn to care for Mabel. Stepping over to Jack, she held her hand out for the sponge he was using to clean the gentle mare.

"Shouldn't I be doing that?"

He considered her proffered hand and raised an eyebrow. "It's the mark of a good horseman to properly care for your horse."

"I'll take that as a yes." She took the wet sponge from him and faced Mabel's flank. "Show me what to do."

He stepped close behind Tracy, covering her hand with his, his chest nestled against her back. "Like this. You want to clean the sweat and dirt left under the saddle," he said, but she could barely hear his instructions over the heady buzzing in her ears. "Do a visual check for sores or other wounds that may need attention."

Cool water rippled down Mabel's sides as Jack guided Tracy's hand in long strokes. When Mabel snuffled and tossed her mane, Jack chuckled. "You like that, girl?"

She couldn't speak for Mabel, but Tracy was enjoying the grooming lesson quite a bit. The press of Jack's body against hers was heavenly. Despite the odors of horse sweat and straw, she caught a hint of the crisp masculine scent that clung to him, a heady blend of soap and spice. He stepped back from her, taking the sponge with him to refresh in the water bucket, and she shook herself from her trance. This time when he handed her the sponge, he stayed where he was, letting her wipe Mabel down without his help.

"That's the way. When you're done with that, you'll

dry her off with the same long strokes." He pointed out a towel waiting on a hook by Mabel's stall. "And when you've finished that, call me, and I'll help you check her hooves for stones or other problems."

He stepped aside, unclipping his cell phone from his belt and thumbing in a number from memory. "Hey, Ryan. It's Jack...yeah, we have a situation out here. At the old Colton cemetery on the north property..." His voice faded as he stalked toward the other end of the stable.

Shuddering at the thought of the skeleton Jack had found, Tracy wiped the perspiration from her temple with her arm, careful to avoid wetting herself with the sponge. Strands of hair fell in her face, and she carefully plucked at them with her damp fingers. She'd need a shower after this for sure.

Greta strolled past and nudged her with an elbow. "Here." She held a ponytail holder on her palm, which Tracy accepted gratefully. "You'll find it's most practical to wear your hair back on the ranch. I have a bunch of these bands up at the house if you want a few."

"Thanks." Tracy contemplated the sponge in one hand and the elastic hair holder in the other for a second before Greta chuckled.

"Let me." Jack's sister took the elastic band back from her and finger-combed Tracy's hair into a respectably neat ponytail. "There." Greta stepped in front of her to inspect her handiwork, and an odd expression crossed her face.

Tracy frowned. "What's wrong? You still thinking about the baby?"

Her new friend shook her head and smiled. "Yes and no. It's just...nice to have another woman around. Being the only female on a ranch full of testosterone-reeking cowboys can get old."

Tracy pulled a face. "Aw, poor Greta. Surrounded by too many good-looking men?"

She snorted. "Most of whom are my brothers, remember."

Tracy shrugged, conceding the point. "Ah, well…"

"But you should enjoy yourself while you're here." Greta waggled her eyebrows at her and flashed a smug grin. "Maybe a little vacation fling?"

"M-me?" The idea flustered Tracy so much, she choked and ended up coughing and gasping for a breath.

Greta laughed and pounded her on the back. "Yes, you. Why not?"

Tracy cast a side glance at Jack, who'd finished his phone call, and found him watching them with a frown.

"Maybe Brett? He's quite the catch, if a bit of a playboy," Greta suggested.

"Um…" Tracy watched Jack's scowl deepen. Was it the idea of her having a fling that upset him, or just the notion she might have one with Brett?

"Or Daniel? Eric… No, he doesn't seem interested in dating. Let's see, I could introduce you to H—"

"Leave her alone, Greta, and stop pimping out your brothers."

"Aw," Greta said with a teasing pout, "is Jackie jealous I didn't suggest him?"

In answer, Jack swatted his sister's butt with the towel he'd used to dry off Buck and shot her an unamused grin. "You're funny."

Greta sauntered away, grinning smugly. "Think about it, Tracy. And I'll see you Thursday for your riding lesson."

Tracy waved to her new friend and turned back to Mabel, all too aware of Jack's gaze on her. Oh, she'd think about a fling, all right. She'd already entertained the notion. Too bad the object of that fantasy seemed too tightly wound, too dead set on challenging her at every turn.

The next morning, after eating a large country-style breakfast with Abra, Big J and Brett, Tracy hitched a ride with Big J down to Jack's house, hoping to beg a favor. He seemed startled to see her and his father on his porch, but he stepped back and waved them inside with a courteous nod.

"Jack," Big J started, "I've been on the phone with Ralph Menger down at First National. We've discussed reallocating some funds for the ranch, and I need you to run into town this afternoon and sign the paperwork."

Jack squared his shoulders. "What sort of reallocations?"

"Don't get your undies in a twist. Just the changes you and I discussed last week. Ralph made some other suggestions, which he'll show you when you go in. I'd go myself, but I didn't sleep well last night, and, well, I'm just feeling a bit off today."

Jack eyed his father with obvious concern. "Maybe Eric should stop by and check your—"

Big J cut him off with a scoff and flapped a hand in dismissal. "Don't bother your brother. He's busy at the hospital, and I don't have a thing wrong with me that a nap and a nip of Maker's Mark won't cure."

Tracy cleared her throat, dragging Jack's worried frown to her. "And I was hoping I could tag along into town. I seem to have brought entirely inappropriate clothes for the ranch, and I'd like to shop for jeans and boots. Maybe some more casual shirts, as well."

Jack scratched his stubble-dusted chin. "Why doesn't Greta take you shopping? Or Abra?"

"Abra is busy, and Greta is in Oklahoma City until

Thursday." Tracy paused, shifting her weight uneasily. "If it's an imposition, maybe I can—"

"No. It's fine." His tone contradicted him, but she didn't argue.

Big J clapped his son on the shoulder. "All right, then. Ralph's expecting you in an hour. Ms. McCain." He tugged the brim of his cowboy hat as he nodded a goodbye to her and opened the door. "Thank you, son."

An awkward silence filled the foyer after Big J left. Jack studied her, his lips twisted in thought.

She glanced into the living room. "Where's Seth? Will he come with us?"

"Is that what this is about? An excuse to see Seth?"

"No," she said with a sigh, getting a bit tired of Jack's paranoia regarding his son. "It's about needing ranch clothes. I was just wondering where Seth is."

"He's getting a riding lesson with Daniel."

"A riding lesson? I thought he did quite well on Pooh yesterday."

"There's more to riding a horse than staying in the saddle. Daniel's likely got him on one of the cutting horses, teaching him some basics about roping."

"A cutting horse? But he's only five years old!"

Jack gave a dismissive shrug. "I learned to ride a cutting horse when I was five. So did Brett. I rode a bull in my first rodeo when I was thirteen."

She shook her head in dismay. "Good gravy!"

He flipped a hand, as if his early start in the dangerous sport was nothing. "Thing is, Daniel won't push Seth past what he's capable of." Jack stepped past her, snagging his black Stetson from a peg on the wall. "Come on, I'll show you."

Tracy followed him out into the ranch yard. Even before they reached the practice pen, she could hear Daniel's whoops and Seth's laughter. Jack stopped at the fence and leaned against a post to watch his son race around the pen on the back of a dark brown horse twice the size of Pooh. Tracy held her breath as Seth wove between barrels and galloped past them. While she hadn't yet been formally introduced to Daniel, she immediately recognized the tall copper-skinned cowboy who'd parked her car the day she'd arrived, the half brother who'd been excluded from Big J's toast to Greta. His teeth flashed white against his dark complexion as he grinned and shouted to Seth. "That's the way, buddy! One more time, and then bring him in."

Tracy nodded her head toward Seth's riding coach. "So Daniel is your half brother?"

"Yep." Jack cut a side look at her. "Who told you that?"

"Greta. She said that Abra is none too happy to have him living on the ranch, but the rest of you consider him family."

"He *is* family. And a damn fine rancher and horseman, too. He's an asset to the ranch, even if my mother can't see it."

Tracy eyed Daniel and his tall, muscular frame. The term "tall, dark and handsome" had surely been coined with Daniel in mind. "Was his mother Hispanic?"

"No. Cherokee."

Jack didn't elaborate on his relationship with Daniel, so Tracy let the subject drop. The tone of his voice as he defended Daniel's status in the Colton clan indicated the affection Jack felt for Big J's illegitimate son.

Once Seth had made another circuit in the ring, he reined the horse and trotted up to Daniel. His uncle lifted him down from the saddle and ruffled his hair. "Well done, partner. You need to work on keeping a firm grip on the reins and controlling your horse, but we'll work on that another day."

"Can I help you cool him down and feed him?" Seth asked eagerly.

"You better," Daniel said, picking Seth up like a sack of potatoes and tucking him under his arm. "I'm not doing all of your dirty work, kid."

Seth squealed in delight as Daniel toted him into one of the horse stalls.

Jack pushed away from the fence, and as they passed the door to the stable, he called, "Daniel, can you keep an eye on Seth for a while? I'm running an errand in town and won't be back for a few hours."

Daniel glanced in their direction and arched a speculative dark eyebrow when he spotted Tracy. He set Seth's feet on the ground before nodding to Jack. "Sure thing. Take your time. All I had planned this afternoon was going over some paperwork with Megan. When I finish that, I'll challenge Shorty here to 'Mario Kart.' It's been a while since I kicked his butt at video games."

"No way!" Seth said with a laugh. "I'll kick *your* butt!"

Jack's lips twitched in a grin, and he tugged the brim of his Stetson. "Thanks, Daniel, I owe you one."

Daniel barked a laugh. "You owe me about twenty, but who's counting?"

Jack took Tracy's elbow and steered her toward the ranch yard. "We should go if I'm expected at the bank in an hour."

"He's good with Seth. Does Daniel have any kids of his own?"

"Naw. Seth is Big J's only grandchild to date. But you're right. Daniel has a good rapport with Seth. He's patient and soft-spoken but firm, which is why he's so good with his horses, too."

Tracy sputtered a chuckle. "Did you just compare your son to a horse?"

"You laugh, but the same traits that make Daniel a good horse trainer will serve him well raising his own kids one day."

"Touché," Tracy conceded, with a last glance over her shoulder to the gentle giant ruffling Seth's hair in the stable.

If Seth was surrounded by the strong, caring role models his uncles and aunt clearly provided, had a father who guarded him and loved him beyond all else, and had the security and joys of his ranch home, what did she really think she had to offer the boy? Maybe she was wrong to try to insert herself into his life. Laura had believed Seth was better off at the Lucky C, even as much as she'd loved her only child. A quiver started low in Tracy's belly. Was her own purpose in being at the ranch misguided? Selfish?

She bit her bottom lip, and as she mulled the question over, she remembered how Seth had gobbled up the attention she'd lavished on him when he'd hurt his hand. His green eyes had been bright with a needy plea, a clear longing for a mother's touch.

Jack might think his young son was capable beyond his years, encouraging Seth to be independent, responsible, and to attempt tasks beyond what Tracy felt a five-year-old should be asked to perform. But she saw the still very little boy. She saw how Seth longed to please his father, saw his need for comfort, care and cuddling. Those things she could provide. Her heart was full of a tender longing to nurture Seth as she would her own child.

She followed Jack to his truck, a mud-splattered F-250 with an extended cab, and eyed the giant step up into the passenger seat with dismay. Not that she couldn't hoist

herself up, but her muscles were still stiff and achy from
the ride yesterday morning.

Seeing her hesitation, Jack twitched a grin and kicked
the running board with his boot. "Use this to step up."

She tipped her head, giving him a how-dumb-do-I-
look glance. "I know *how* to climb up. I'm just dreading
it. My legs are rather sore from yesterday."

"Understandable." He put a hand under her elbow,
and a crackling awareness shimmied through her. "I'll
give ya a boost."

His grip was warm and firm, and his spare hand
rested at her back, steadying her. Sparks raced through
her blood, and her breath caught. She flashed back to
the last boost he'd given her, when he'd palmed her behind. Many more helping hands from Jack, and she'd be
a puddle of goo. After he'd closed the door, she released
the breath she held in a tremulous gush. Who was this
giddy schoolgirl she became in Jack's company?

The ride into Tulsa took about twenty-five minutes.
Tracy tried to engage Jack in conversation, curious
to learn more about the man her cousin had married.
Though he answered all her questions willingly enough,
his responses were terse, often no more than a yes or no.
She'd hoped that if she and Jack got to know each other
better, he'd loosen up a bit about her spending time with
Seth.

"Will Seth start kindergarten in the fall?" she asked,
clutching the passenger armrest as he took the tight turn
of an interstate exit ramp.

His expression hardened. "No."

"Why not? He's five, isn't he?"

"Yeah, but I'm holding him out until next year."

She frowned. "Why would you do that?"

Jack gave her a peevish look. "Because I'm his father, and don't think he's ready."

Tracy blinked, surprised at this. By all indications, Seth was unusually bright, inquisitive and extremely verbal. "Is it Seth that's not ready for kindergarten...or you?"

Jack's face grew darker as he glanced at her while negotiating traffic. "What does that mean?"

"He certainly seems ready for school to me. How can you think he's old enough to ride a cutting horse but not go to kindergarten?"

Jack squeezed the steering wheel tighter and cut her an irritated glare. "They're totally different."

She gnawed her lip as she studied him. "I can't help but wonder... Does your decision mean you're not ready for him to grow up? Maybe you want to keep him under your wing another year before letting him leave the ranch all day?"

A muscle in Jack's jaw flexed as he gritted his teeth. "And maybe you're overstepping your boundaries. I know what's best for Seth."

She raised a conceding hand. "My apologies. I only mean to say he seems intellectually advanced for his age to me. Probably because he spends so much time around adults."

Jack's mouth pressed in a grim line. "Is that another criticism?"

"No! Not at all. I think it is wonderful Seth has so many uncles and Greta to dote on him. I think it's contributed to his verbal skills and curiosity."

Jack stopped at a red light and bumped the steering wheel with his fist. "Edith thinks I should send him to school in September. She thinks he needs to be around kids his own age."

"I have to agree." Tracy paused, racking her memory. "Who is Edith, again?"

"The housekeeper at the main house. She was more mother to us growing up than Abra was. Abra traveled a lot when we were kids, and Edith helped our nannies. Now she helps me out with Seth."

"Oh. So she would know what she's talking about." When he turned to her with an impatient scowl, Tracy added quickly, "I know you don't care what I think, but... have you asked Seth what he wants?"

Jack's expression said that he not only had never considered Seth's opinion about school, he was taken aback by her suggestion. A car behind them honked, and Jack gave the truck more gas than needed, zipping across the intersection as he cast her a disgruntled look.

"I'm not saying leave the decision to him. You have the final say as his parent, but you should feel him out. Don't make him promises or give him false expectations, just ask him general questions to gauge his interest and needs. Does he ever miss having friends his age to play with? Is he curious about books and learning how to write?"

"I think I know my son."

Jack's sarcastic tone stung, and she turned toward the passenger window. "I'm sorry. I was just trying to help."

Across the truck cab, she heard Jack groan. "No, I'm sorry. You didn't deserve that. I get...touchy when I feel like someone is second-guessing me. I make the choices I feel are best regarding the running of the ranch and raising my son, and when someone questions my intentions or decisions, I..." He huffed a sigh.

She swiveled to face him, studying the shadows in his expression. The crease in his brow said he had more than just their discussion about when Seth would start school on his mind. "Are you concerned about this banking business Big J asked you to handle?"

Jack flicked a startled look to her. "I—no, that's not… Well, maybe a little, but it's not the main thing on my plate at the moment."

She watched him fidget and drum his thumbs on the steering wheel for a minute or two, and finally asked, "Want to talk about it?"

He dented his brow and frowned at her. "No."

"Mmm, well…if you change your mind, I'm a good listener. I'll even promise not to offer any advice."

He snorted and sent her a skeptical grin. "Yeah, right."

She gave him a playful slug in the arm in return. Which was a mistake, because feeling the firm bulge of muscle under his sleeve only refreshed the tingle of lustful awareness she'd been trying to tamp down.

Jack parked his truck in front of the bank and sat staring out the windshield for a moment before cutting the engine. "Brett wants me to invest in horse breeding. He's found a stud he thinks we should buy to start a breeding program that Daniel would run. When I said no the first time, he went out lobbying investors to front the cash. I shut that down the other day, but I know he hasn't forgotten the subject. He thinks breeding cutting horses will make us a buttload of profit and entice Daniel to stay at the Lucky C instead of starting his own breeding business."

Tracy blinked. *You asked*, she thought.

She wet her lips and chose her words carefully, determined not to blow this opportunity. Jack had trusted her enough to confide his business worries, and she hated to jeopardize that by saying the wrong thing.

Before she got the chance to say anything, right or wrong, he aimed his thumb down the street. "There are clothing stores that way. Laura dragged me shopping with her a few times and had some luck at a few shops the next block down. If you turn down the block to the right there's a department store that way, too."

Tracy peered at the signs along the street and got a sense of her options. "And where do you suggest I get a pair of basic jeans for the ranch?"

Jack cracked an amused half grin. "Feed and seed store."

She hummed a wry acknowledgment, enjoying the more affable tone between them. "Where and when shall we meet?"

He lifted a shoulder. "Don't know. I could be an hour or more."

She pulled her cell phone from her purse. "What's your number?"

They exchanged mobile numbers, and he told her he'd text when he was finished with his bank business. Sliding her sunglasses on, Tracy climbed out of Jack's truck and started down the sidewalk. The June heat had already swelled to stifling levels, and made the fumes of exhaust from the many cars all the more suffocating. She did a bit of window shopping as she strolled, admiring artwork at galleries, tempting pastries at a bakery and sparkling rings and pendants at a high-end jeweler. When she reached a shop with cowboy boots and stylish Western shirts on the mannequins in the display window, she stepped inside, sighing in pleasure as the store's air-conditioning bathed her heated face.

She greeted the shopkeeper and began searching the racks of women's jeans and shirts, finding numerous items she thought would work. Most of the clothes she tried on were affordable, and from the clearance table she scored a great pair of no-frills boots that would be perfect for the ranch yard and stables. After paying for her purchases—two pairs of jeans, the boots and one Western button-down shirt—she headed back out in search of more bargains. Spending Cliff's life-insurance money always reminded her that soon she'd have to find a job. Not that she had a problem with that. But because Cliff had refused to let her work, she hadn't been in the workforce for a long time. She'd be playing catch-up, learning the latest technology and software wherever she landed.

As she strolled down the sidewalk, glancing in store windows, a strange sensation crawled up her spine. She knew the spiders-up-her-back feeling well, had finetuned the sixth sense during her marriage to Cliff. A premonition. A warning. She stiffened, and a chill washed through her, despite the muggy heat.

Someone was watching her. Maybe it was Jack, she thought, trying to be optimistic. Hadn't she felt an odd sort of connection to him? But her link to Jack didn't give her this creepy sensation.

Casting a surreptitious glance to the reflection of the busy street in the display window beside her, Tracy looked for signs of anything suspicious. She studied the reflection but didn't see Jack or anyone else watching her. Turning slowly, she lowered her sunglasses to better view the people on the street. The prickling sensation eased, and Tracy chalked the feeling up to lingering paranoia. Spending Cliff's life-insurance money brought the realities of her doomed marriage up from the recesses of her memory. His control over her had included their finances, and she'd had to account for every penny she'd spent. If her purchases didn't meet with his approval, she'd paid the price physically and in humiliation.

But Cliff was dead. She was free of his tyranny and cruelty.

Shake it off. She rolled the tension from her shoulders and wiped the sheen of sweat from her upper lip. Since Jack hadn't yet texted that he was finished with his business, she headed to the next block of stores and found a boutique with pretty shoes and fun jewelry. Not ranch attire, for sure, but intriguing to browse through. She found a pair of shorts she wanted and some pumps to replace the ones she'd ruined her first day at the ranch.

Her cell phone buzzed as she was signing the credit card receipt at the boutique, and Tracy glanced at the screen.

All done. Meet at truck.

Tucking her phone back in her purse, she thanked the shop attendant and bustled out onto the sidewalk, headed back to meet Jack with her purchases. She smiled to herself, satisfied with the success of the trip. From a block away, she spotted Jack's black cowboy hat. He was leaning against the front of his truck, his legs crossed in front of him in a relaxed pose as he waited for her. She thought of how her new shorts showed off her legs and wondered what Jack would think of her new acquisition. Her stomach bunched with a giddy thrill as she imagined Jack's green gaze studying her with a hint of heat and promise.

Tracy stopped at the street corner, waiting for the light to change and traffic to clear before she crossed. She couldn't wait to get in the—

A large hand struck her back. Shoved.

Tracy gasped as she reeled forward. Her arms windmilled, and her bags scattered as she stumbled off the curb. A car horn blasted. A bumper smacked her legs, and she heard brakes screech, tires squeal. She slammed to the pavement with a tooth-jarring impact.

Chapter 7

For several mind-numbing seconds, Tracy lay sprawled on the scorching concrete. She couldn't catch her breath. Couldn't hear over the whoosh of blood pounding in her ears. Finally, the fog of shock cleared, and she made a quick assessment of her condition. Her knees stung. Her hip throbbed. Her hands burned.

An engine roared. A car whizzed past, narrowly missing her head. She was in the street, blocking traffic. People had begun to gather around her, touching her shoulder, asking her questions. Was she all right? Did she need an ambulance?

She shuddered as adrenaline coursed through her. "I—I th-think I'm—"

"Tracy!" The deep voice reverberated through her, curling warmly inside her like a smooth shot of whiskey.

She blinked against the bright sun as she glanced up at the rugged face of the speaker looming over her. *Jack*. His dark eyebrows were knit, his eyes lit with concern.

"J-Jack…" She tried to stand, tried to dust the grit from her seared palms, but her legs ached and buckled when she attempted to rise from the pavement. A pair of strong arms caught her when she swayed, lifting her, cradling her against a broad chest.

"I've got you," he murmured against her hair. Someone had gathered her bags and handed them to Jack, hooking them on his fingers. He juggled both her and her purchases as he headed down the street.

Safe. The word flittered through her mind. The instant he pulled her close, a sense of security rolled through her that went beyond that street corner and her tumble into traffic. Her muscles relaxed, and her bones seemed to melt as she leaned into Jack's embrace. Her galloping pulse slowed to an even canter.

Jack moved away from the crowded corner and carried her toward his pickup. "Are you hurt?"

"N-no. Just shaken up. I don't know what happened. I—"

He chuckled softly. "Clearly, you tripped. Not surprising, given all these bags."

She flattened her hand against his chest, savoring the low rumble.

And then she remembered the hand at her back, the shove. Fresh adrenaline rushed through her. Her gut twisted, and her body shuddered. Someone had pushed her into traffic. Heartlessly. Viciously. Intentionally.

She gasped, and her fingers curled into Jack's shirt. "Oh my God."

"What?" Beneath the brim of his cowboy hat, his brow dented.

"I didn't trip. I—I was pushed."

He grunted. "Accidents happen."

"No." She shook her head as a chill crept through her. "I mean someone shoved me. On purpose."

He arched a dark eyebrow. "On purpose?" He gave a short, snorting laugh. "Paranoid much?"

His skepticism sliced to her core. In the wake of the warm comfort she'd experienced moments earlier, his doubt seemed all the more sharp and cold. "I'm not imagining things. I felt a hand push me. Hard."

They'd reached his F-250, and he shifted her bags, trying to open the passenger door.

"You can put me down. I can stand alone now."

He stooped to ease her legs to the ground, and she winced as her hip bore her full weight again. Jack didn't move away until she steadied herself and gave him a nod.

"You should see a doctor."

She glanced down at her scraped palms. While they stung and she was sure she'd have a nasty bruise on her hip, she didn't feel the injuries warranted a doctor's care. "No, I'll be all right."

Jack grunted and narrowed a scrutinizing gaze on her. "Why?"

She blinked at him as she took her bags back. "What?"

"Why would someone push you?" He flipped the bucket seat forward, then loaded her purchases on the backseat.

"I don't know. But…" Tracy paused and frowned. "You think I'm lying? Why would I lie about it?"

"I didn't say that. But maybe you mistook an accidental bump as a push. That makes more sense than someone gunning for you."

She blew on her palms, which throbbed more now that the adrenaline from her tumble had subsided. "I know what I felt."

"Well, I wasn't watching you the whole time, but…I

didn't see anyone specific come up behind you. If someone *had* pushed you, don't you think someone would have seen them and said something?"

"I saw him," a woman on the sidewalk said.

Tracy whipped her gaze toward the petite woman with glasses. "You did?"

"I did." The woman nodded and pushed wispy hair back from her face. "He was a big guy, but for his size he moved quickly. He pushed you, and in the hullabaloo of your fall, he disappeared."

Jack tapped the brim of his Stetson back as he faced the woman. "What did he look like?"

"Well…" The woman screwed her face up in thought. "It was an older white man." She twisted her lips as if unsure, then added, "I mean, I assume he was older. He had a lot of gray hair, anyway. The rest was dark. And like I said, he was really big. Not just tall, but big all over. Dark clothes. That's all I remember."

Tracy should have felt vindicated, having the woman's confirmation. Instead, her gut roiled and her apprehension grew. Someone had targeted her, tried to hurt her. Jack's question reverberated in her head. Why? Why would someone want to hurt her?

"I just came over to make sure you were okay," the woman said. She waved a finger toward Tracy. "You need to clean those scrapes so they don't get infected. Do you have hand sanitizer?"

Tracy tried to answer, but a belated reaction to the man's attack snaked through her and left her numb and trembling.

"I have a first-aid box in my truck, and I'm taking her to the ER, just in case." Jack's voice cut through her distraction, and he put a hand at her elbow to assist her into the truck.

She roused from her daze with a jolt. The ER? The urgent-care department at hospitals held too many memories of trips for injuries when she'd "tripped over the dog" or "slipped on the ice." Her most recent visit to the ER had been the worst. Laura had been pronounced DOA. Cliff had arrived in a separate ambulance, barely scraped. And Tracy had sustained a broken collarbone, bruising to her face and internal injuries that required a week's stay in a Denver hospital. She swallowed hard, forcing down the bitter taste that rose in her throat.

"No, Jack, please…no hospital," she pleaded.

"My brother works at Tulsa General. I'll call and have him meet us."

When she shook her head, a lightning-like streak of pain shot under her skull. She drew a sharp breath and raised a hand to her screaming temple.

"Humph," Jack grunted. "See? No arguments."

The ER. She hugged her arms to her chest as Jack circled the truck and climbed behind the wheel. Images flashed in her mind's eye, and whispers of ancient shouts hissed in her ear. Cliff's derision. His slaps. His fingers biting into her arm. She thought she'd escaped that brand of fear. Laura had died helping to free her.

Jack cranked the engine and turned the air conditioner on high. Reaching across her, he opened the glove box and took out a plastic box.

If Cliff was dead, who was the man targeting her today?

Jack handed her the first-aid kit. "Here. I keep this in here for accidents when I'm out in the pastures. You can waste a lot of time driving back to the house to treat every cut and scrape you get while ranching. This is a start, but I want Eric to check you for concussion." He started the engine, then paused, narrowing a hard look at her. "Tracy, what is it? You look like you've seen a ghost."

In a manner of speaking, she had. "I—I just can't imagine why someone would want to hurt me. Who would w-want to do this?"

Jack shook his head. "I still think you're making assumptions. You don't know you were targeted. The man that woman described may have bumped you, but that doesn't mean he singled you out, to harm you."

She angled her head to meet Jack's gaze, to reiterate her case, but stopped. His words said he didn't believe her, but his eyes were full of doubts and turmoil.

Over the next several minutes, she protested his decision to take her to the hospital many times, but Jack headed straight to the emergency room, where his brother Eric met them at the entrance with a wheelchair. She felt a bit self-conscious using the wheelchair, but when she tried to climb out of the truck, her body throbbed and she stumbled. Jack caught her arm and eased her into the seat.

"Missy, set them up in exam room three, please." At his bidding, a nurse scurried ahead of them down a side hall. Eric wasted no time hustling Tracy through the lobby. "What happened, Jack?"

Jack explained how she'd fallen into the street, leaving out her allegation that she'd been pushed, and outlined his concerns about a head injury and significant contusions. Eric parked the wheelchair in the room where the nurse was waiting, then lifted Tracy from the seat onto the exam table. Like his brother's, Eric's arms were strong and steady, his chest broad, but she didn't get the same deep-down sense of security that Jack's hold had given her.

"This is all unnecessary. Really." She tried again, but like his brother, Eric ignored her protest. While the nurse took her blood pressure, Eric began a meticulous examination of her pupils, the injuries to her hands and knees.

She sat quietly through the exam, giving Jack's brother her own brand of scrutiny. Though Tracy saw the obvious facial similarities, Jack's brother wore his lighter brown hair in a buzz cut instead of the shaggy style Jack did. Jack had introduced him as his younger brother, but Eric seemed older than Jack in several ways. Foremost was the fact that he had tiny creases around his eyes and bracketing his mouth. On someone else, the fine lines would have detracted from his appearance, but on Eric, the creases enhanced the chiseled intensity of his handsome face. Eric's Colton-green eyes had a much more serious look that reflected his gravitas as he treated his patient. With a gentle touch, he palpated her scalp, and she winced when he found a tender spot.

"Missy, will you arrange for a CT scan?" Eric asked, without looking up from his study of Tracy's injuries.

"Of course, Dr. Colton."

Tracy cut a glance to the nurse as she lifted the receiver on an in-house phone. Tracy noted that the nurse's attention never left Eric as she made the call. The young woman's expression was openly worshipful, leaving no question that she was smitten with the doctor. Not that Tracy blamed the gal. She'd yet to meet a Colton male who was less than drool worthy.

"Does this hurt?" Eric asked her as he flexed her wrist.

She shifted her attention back to Jack's brother, who seemed oblivious to the nurse's admiring gaze. "Not much. Just a—oh!" She gasped as a bolt of pain shot up her arm.

Eric grunted. "Let's get her wrist x-rayed, as well."

"Yes, Doctor." Missy all but swooned when he glanced at her.

Another nurse passed the open door to the exam room and did a double take as she glanced in. She pulled up short and stepped inside, pasting a smile on her lips. "Dr. Colton, I didn't know you were working the ER today."

"I'm not. I'm just helping my brother out with an emergency." Eric never glanced up as he cleaned and disinfected Tracy's scraped knee.

"Oh, can I do anything to help?" The nurse smiled and squared her shoulders in such a way that her ample bosom was thrust forward in a none-too-subtle move.

Eric either didn't notice or didn't care about the attractive woman's flirting. The scenario was repeated when a radiology tech arrived to take Tracy for her scans. The women postured and flaunted their wares, but Eric remained focused on his job, apparently immune to the women's attention.

Jack accompanied her to the X-ray lab, and when they were alone she whispered, "Do women always fall over themselves for your brother like that?"

He snorted. "Yeah."

"I can understand. He's quite handsome."

Jack gave her a disgruntled look, one that said he was irritated that she'd noticed his brother's appearance. "They're wasting their time. Eric is all about the job. He's probably the best trauma surgeon in the state, and he's not about to compromise that for a workplace romance."

Tracy had little time to puzzle over Jack's curious reaction to her comment before she was escorted back for her CT scan and X-ray. An hour later, she was discharged with a diagnosis of a strained wrist, which Eric skillfully bandaged with a brace, but no skull fracture. Eric gave her a low-dose shot of Demerol for pain and a prescription for Lorcet for her aches in the coming days, along with instructions to keep her scrapes clean and disin-

fected with over-the-counter ointments. Jack helped her
to the hospital pharmacy to fill her prescription and buy
a supply of antibiotic cream before heading for home.

The drive back to the ranch was largely quiet. Jack cast
frequent side glances to her, until she finally muttered
groggily, "I'm fine. Just woozy. The shot your brother
gave me is making me sleepy."

"Good. You should rest. Close your eyes. I'll wake you
when we get home."

She rocked her head from side to side, the drugs in
her blood making it feel thick and heavy. "I can wait
until we get back."

By the time they returned to the Lucky C, Tracy was
physically and mentally exhausted. Jack helped carry her
bags into the main house, dropping them on the marble
floor at the base of the wide staircase. Before he left, he
gave her a stern appraisal. "I can have Maria send a tray
up with dinner."

"Not necessary. I don't want to be any more of a bother."

He arched an eyebrow, silently communicating his
skepticism.

She bent to gather her bags, biting her bottom lip to
hold back the grunt of discomfort, and wobbling from
the painkiller. When she turned and contemplated negotiating the massive staircase, she couldn't help the fa-
tigued sigh that escaped. Before she could take the first
step, Jack wrapped his fingers around her good wrist and
tugged the bags from her grasp.

"I'll come back and get those," he said, when she
raised a startled look to him. He bent to catch her behind the knees and across her back, then scooped her up
to cradle her against his chest.

Tracy gasped in surprise and clutched his shoulders
for balance. "Jack, what are you doing?"

"I'd think that was obvious."

He started up the steps two at a time, and she had no choice but to lean into him and hold on. With her arms looped around his neck, she buried her face in his shoulder and inhaled the masculine scents of soap and leather that clung to him. As a little girl watching *Gone with the Wind*, she'd swooned when Rhett carried Scarlett up the grand staircase. But Tracy's girlish response to Rhett's act of passion paled now as her head swam dizzily over Jack's valiant gesture. His hold was strong and sure, his stride unfaltering. When he reached the top of the steps, he wasn't even breathing hard.

He swept down the hallway with her, hesitating only long enough to ask, "Which room?"

She raised her muzzy head from the soft fabric of his shirt and met his mesmerizing eyes. Her fingers curled into the shaggy hair on his nape, savoring the silky feel of the wisps against her skin. "Second door on the right."

Jack shouldered his way into the guest room and set her on the sleigh bed. Perhaps it was the drugs lowering her inhibitions, but as she released her grip on him, she allowed her hand to trail slowly from his neck along his shoulder, then linger briefly on his chest. She could feel the steady thump of his heart beneath her palm, and her own pulse answered with hard, clamoring beats.

Glancing up at him with a shaky smile, she shifted her touch to his upper arm, giving a small squeeze of appreciation.

"Thank you." Her voice sounded far too breathy and sensual, as if she were trying to seduce him, and she winced mentally. Clearly, he heard what she had, because his muscles tensed and something hot and hungry flared in his eyes. The predatory gleam in his gaze backed the air up in her lungs and doubled her heart rate. Her ach-ing limbs and stinging wounds were forgotten as she held his stare for what seemed simultaneously an aeon and a flicker in time. Tracy couldn't tell how much of her light-headed buzz was Jack's effect on her and how much was the painkiller, but her head spun dizzily, nonetheless.

When she wet her dry lips, his focus dropped to her mouth, and his pupils grew to inky, fathomless pools. She both hoped and feared that he was going to kiss her. His desire was evident in the intensity of his stare and the quiver in his muscles as he hovered over her. A shiver of expectation sluiced through her.

In the end, though, he clenched his jaw and shoved away from the bed with an exhalation rife with frustration. Disappointment rippled through Tracy, and she sank deeper into the pillows, kicking herself for wanting things she shouldn't. How could she be lusting after her cousin's ex when she was still coping with the aftermath of her own late husband?

"I'll get your bags," Jack said as he stalked from her room, his tone deeper and huskier than usual. From unspent desire? she wondered. Within minutes, fatigue dragged her into a deep sleep and dreams of Jack carrying her through a swirling flood of black water.

The next morning, a thunderstorm woke Tracy. When a particularly close crash rattled the guest room windows, Tracy bolted upright in her bed and raked her hair back from her face. Her bedside alarm clock read 6:24 a.m. Knowing that the rest of the ranch residents were likely up and starting their day, Tracy tossed back the covers and staggered to the shower. Her muscles were predictably sore and stiff, and the hot water stung her healing scrapes. All in all, she knew she was lucky to be alive. If she'd fallen in traffic just as a vehicle sped by, she'd have a lot more than stiff muscles to worry about.

After her shower, Tracy joined Abra for breakfast in the formal dining room.

"I understand you had some excitement yesterday," Abra said.

So Jack had shared news of her accident with the family. Tracy rolled her sore shoulders. "You could call it that, just…not the kind of excitement one likes to have."

"But Eric got you all fixed up?"

"Yes, ma'am. He and Jack were both very helpful."

Abra smiled brightly. "I have no doubt."

Tracy passed the plate of scrambled eggs to her hostess. "What time will Greta be back today?"

"Somewhere around three this afternoon, I believe." Abra pulled a face and shook her head. "Honestly, I think she should go ahead and move to Oklahoma City, rather than commute back and forth as she plans the wedding. But she hates to leave her horses. Sometimes I think she loves the horses more than she does Mark."

Tracy grinned, assuming that Abra was teasing, but the crease in Abra's forehead said otherwise.

When Big J arrived in the dining room, he greeted Tracy with a warm smile. "You all right this morning, darlin'?"

She showed him her raw palms and wrapped wrist with a grimace. "A little dinged up, but nothing I can't handle. Still planning to make the most of the day."

He tipped his hat to her. "That's the cowboy spirit."

Abra invited Big J to join them for breakfast, but he only poured a cup coffee and took a piece of bacon with him as he left for the stables. Tracy sensed an awkwardness between them and recalled what Greta had said about Big J's indiscretion with Daniel's mother, and

Jack's comment that Abra had traveled most of his child-hood. None of her business, Tracy told herself as she nibbled her bacon.

A loud clap of thunder shook the house hard enough to make the china coffee cups on the table rattle. Abra frowned, as if the storm was insulting her personally. "What plans do you have today? This weather looks to keep us inside for a while."

Tracy cupped her hands around her mug of java, sa-voring the rich aroma. "I brought a book to read, but if you have something I can help you with, I'd be happy to."

Abra lifted a shoulder. "No. I have a few calls to make for the wedding, thank-you notes to write."

After taking a gulp of coffee, Tracy pushed her eggs around her plate, wondering what Jack and his son were up to this rainy morning. "I'd like to spend some time with Seth today. Maybe we could play cards or a board game. Do you think Jack would bring him up to the house?"

Abra gave another mild shrug. "You're welcome to call him. Jack's house is number two on speed dial." She nodded toward the landline telephone on the kitchen wall.

"Oh, thanks, but I have his cell number on my phone."

Abra quirked an eyebrow, clearly intrigued and read-ing hidden meaning into that fact, but she made no com-ment.

Tracy managed to keep up a stilted conversation with Abra through the rest of breakfast, but when she finished eating, she excused herself to her room. As she walked along the upstairs corridor, she passed one of the mul-lioned windows that looked out over the front lawn and circular drive leading to the front door. She lingered long enough to enjoy the view, made all the more enticing when a golden ray of sun peeked through the departing rain clouds. On the lawn below, near a side door of the house, she spotted a familiar head of wavy brown hair and long willowy limbs.

Tracy blinked, startled to see Greta at the ranch. Had she gotten back early? Abra had said she wasn't expected until closer to three.

Tracy raised her hand to knock on the window and wave to Greta, but the woman below gave a furtive glance over her shoulder, then darted in the side door, out of view.

Odd. Maybe Greta's business in OKC had been cut short. Or, Tracy decided, noting how the decorative glass made slight distortions to the view, maybe it hadn't been Greta at all, but a member of the household staff who had a similar hairstyle.

Dismissing the incident, Tracy continued down the long hall to the guest room, where she cracked open the windows to enjoy the cool breeze and pattering of the last drips of rain. She put away the clothes she'd bought yesterday, setting aside a pair of jeans to wear to her riding lesson this evening with Greta.

Once the morning downpour cleared, leaving the air smelling sweet and clean, Tracy decided to enjoy her novel by the pool. She changed into shorts and a tank top, then trooped down to the patio and dragged a lounge chair into the sun near the deep end of the pool. As Tracy stretched out on the lounge chair, her muscles protested with a dull ache. She thought about the bottle of prescription painkillers on her bedside table but didn't like the idea of using the potent medicine unless she *really* needed it.

Leaning her head back, she closed her eyes behind her sunglasses and recalled the muzzy feeling the Demerol shot had given her last night...and the way her drug-muddled brain had led her to act. Her cheeks heated as she remembered how she'd draped herself over Jack, caressing his face and all but simpering for a kiss. Even now her head spun, thinking about the rough scrape of his day-end beard against her fingers and the hooded look of wanting in his eyes. How could she face him after her awkward advances?

Exhaling a cleansing breath, she tipped her head farther back and savored the warmth of the morning sun. She must have dozed off, because the next thing she was aware of was the slapping sound of running feet, then a loud splash. Fat drops of cold water rained down on her sun-baked skin, and she jerked upright with a gasp. Now fully awake, she shielded her eyes from the sun to bring the pool into focus. A small dark head broke the surface near her, and Seth grinned up at her, spiky lashes surrounding green eyes full of mischief.

"Did I splash ya?" he asked, with no sign of remorse.

She gave him a playful scowl and shook water droplets off her book. "You did. Scamp."

He wrinkled his nose. "What's a scamp?"

"A little boy who splashes unsuspecting ladies, then grins about it." She gave him a lopsided smile and a mock growl.

He laughed and padded away, calling, "Wanna swim with me?"

"Maybe later. I'm feeling kinda sore and stiff after my fall yesterday."

He grabbed the rail of the ladder at the deep end and cocked his head. "Daddy says you tripped and fell in the street. I bet that hurt. Did ya skin your hands and knees? I do that a lot."

Tripped, huh? She supposed the filtered version was better for Seth. Best not to worry the boy needlessly.

She held up her hands and bandaged wrist to show him. "A little scraped. But I've had worse. Just sore today."

Seth poked at a beetle floating in the water. "Daddy says the best thing to do when you're sore is work it out. Layin' round will just make ya stiff."

"Oh, he does, does he?" She could imagine Jack saying this to motivate his son to put away his video games or TV and get out in the fresh air. Hearing Seth parrot his father brought a secret smile to her lips that she bit her cheek to squelch.

Jack's son nodded. "It works, too. When I get sore from ridin' Pooh or mucking stalls, I take a walk, and I'm all better the next day."

She didn't bother to argue that his resilience probably had more to do with his youth than his father's prescribed walks. Instead, she nodded. "That's great, Seth. Maybe I'll try that later."

He hoisted himself out of the pool and padded to her, dripping. "Whatcha reading?"

She showed him the cover of her book. "A romance novel."

Seth screwed up his face. "Romance? Does that mean there's kissin' and stuff?"

Tracy chuckled at his look of disgust. "Yeah. Kissing is part of romance."

"Ew. Kissing is gross!"

She tweaked the boy's nose. "Not if you're doing it right."

With effort, she kept her thoughts from straying to her near kiss with Jack last night. She could well imagine he was an excellent kisser. Knowing how he liked to take control of every situation, she could guess he'd take command of a kiss and leave his partner breathless and satisfied.

"Brett says someday I'll want to kiss girls, same as he does," Seth said, bringing her out of her musing.

"He's right."

"Daddy says I got plenty of time before I gotta worry about kissing girls."

Tracy gave a lopsided grin. "He's right, too."

As if conjured by their discussion, Jack rode up to the back lawn astride Buck and gave a shrill whistle. "Seth, what are you doing up here? I thought you were going to help us sort the calves."

The boy's face brightened. "Oh, yeah. I forgot."

Jack tapped back the brim of his black cowboy hat to send Tracy an appraising scrutiny. She was prepared for him to grouse about her being alone with Seth without his approval, but instead he asked, "How are you feeling this morning?"

The thoroughness of his gaze and the piercing intensity of his eyes were as intimate as a physical caress. Goose bumps rose on her skin, and her breath hitched. She needed a moment to gather her composure before stuttering, "I'm, um, some b-better."

He jerked a nod. "Good." Turning toward his son, he added, "Let's go, Spud. You have to dry off and change clothes, and you're wastin' daylight."

When Seth scampered over to Buck, Jack took his foot from the stirrup, allowing his son to use it for a step up. Jack caught Seth's arm and helped swing him onto Buck's back.

Wrapping one arm around his father from behind, Seth gave her a wave. "'Bye, Miss Tracy. See ya later!"

She returned the wave, and her heart gave a giddy flutter when Jack tapped his hat brim and gave her a nod in parting. Dear Lord, the man was sexy enough without embodying every tough-guy cowboy ideal she remembered from movies. He had the strong and silent archetype down to a tee. Perhaps she couldn't understand Laura's leaving the Lucky C, but Tracy had no problem understanding why her cousin had fallen for Jack Colton to start with.

Chapter 8

"We can do this another day if you're too sore," Greta offered later that evening, as they led Mabel and Scout into the corral for Tracy's riding lesson.

"No, I'm game to give it a try." Tracy found that she'd been looking forward to her riding lesson, partly because she'd enjoyed her last time in the saddle and partly because she enjoyed Greta's company. "I'd wager aches and pains are all part of life for a rancher. If my hosts can work through the pain, so can I."

Greta laughed. "That's the spirit!"

After opening the gate to the corral, Greta tugged Scout's lead, and Tracy followed, guiding Mabel in the somewhat muddy space. "So did things go well in Oklahoma City?"

Lifting her shoulder in dismissal, Greta closed the gate behind them and patted Mabel on the rump as she walked passed. "Well enough. We were interviewed for the society page of the *Journal Record*. Mark was named one of Oklahoma City's most eligible bachelors a couple of years ago, so apparently it's big news that he's getting married." She grinned as she unhooked Mabel's lead and tossed it over a fence post. "Abra was thrilled when I told her about the article, but personally, I find all the attention our wedding is getting a bit overwhelming."

"Your mother did seem to be enjoying the limelight at your engagement party." Tracy shooed a fly that buzzed in her face.

Greta gave a snorting sort of laugh. "Yes, God love her, my mother is happiest when she's the center of attention. My wedding would be a bigger media circus than Prince William and Catherine's royal wedding if I let her have her way. The best thing to come out of this wedding so far is that I've gotten closer to my mother. Being her only daughter, I think she was hoping for someone a little less…well, *tomboyish* than I've been. Being allowed to help me choose a dress and flowers and china patterns has tickled her pink."

"Well, if there's anything I can do to help you with your wedding plans, please ask. I'd be happy to do anything I can."

Greta angled a startled look at her that morphed into a warm smile. "Thank you, Tracy. I appreciate that." She stroked her horse's flank, then sighed. "As much as I love my brothers, I've really missed having a sister. When I saw the camaraderie my brothers had, I always felt like I was missing out on something, not having a sister to share things."

Tracy nodded, swiping perspiration from her brow with the back of her hand. "I can understand that. I was an only child, and I wished I had siblings quite often, too."

"Well, enough of that!" Greta waved off the discussion, which was turning too serious. "Let's get you in the saddle, shall we?" She directed Tracy to a small platform with steps, telling her to walk Mabel up beside the three-foot-high deck. "It's easier for beginners and short people to mount from there."

"Oh." Tracy's cheeks heated when she remembered the intimate boost Jack had given her as she'd climbed into the saddle earlier in the week.

Once Tracy was astride, Greta instructed her to simply walk the perimeter of the corral, getting accustomed to using the reins to guide Mabel. Tracy had opted to wear the gloves Greta had offered, to protect her scraped hands, and she flexed her fingers a few times, loosening the fit. After the first few circuits, Greta joined her, falling in beside Tracy at an easy pace.

"So what's next on your agenda for the wedding? I meant what I said about helping."

"I'll remember that when the time comes to start addressing envelopes. We have hundreds to do!"

Tracy gulped. "Hundreds?"

Greta gave her a wry look. "Heaven forbid Abra leave out anyone she ever met. I told you this wedding was overwhelming." She huffed in frustration, then said, "Next up is a lot of tedious paperwork including the prenup and having our blood tests done for the marriage license. Hardly the fun part of getting married. I much preferred the day we sampled cakes and hors d'oeuvres with the caterers."

Tracy flashed a grin. "I guess so!" She sobered then, and Greta caught her scowl.

"What's that frown for?"

"Well, I guess it just bothers me to hear people talk about getting a prenup. I mean, I can understand why some people feel they're necessary, but…it seems to me if you're marrying someone, it's because you love and trust them. And if that's really the case, a prenup agreement wouldn't be needed." Tracy furrowed her brow. "Is that totally naive of me?"

"Well, I agree with your sentiments, but I didn't want to rock the boat when Mark suggested it. I really have no designs on his money, and when my father heard about the prenup, he was all for it and for protecting my interests in the Lucky C."

Tracy dropped her gaze and shook her head. "I shouldn't have said anything. It's not my business."

"Oh, it's all right." Greta flapped a hand in dismissal. "I know you mean well. After all, signing papers that prepare for a divorce isn't the most romantic way to prepare for a wedding." She pointed to a line of barrels at the end of the corral. "This time go to the left of the first barrel and weave through the others."

Tracy did as instructed, and Greta cheered. "Well done! You're a natural. Now let's pick up the pace." She showed Tracy how to use her legs and stirrups to keep from bouncing in the saddle.

When they paused for a breath, Tracy rubbed the achy muscles in her thighs and lifted a hesitant glance to Greta. She remembered Abra's comment about Greta loving her horses more than her fiancé, and couldn't shake the odd niggling that tickled her brain. "May I be presumptuous one last time?"

Her new friend sent her a wary look, then a wry grin. "Sure. The more candid the better."

"Be sure, before you say 'I do.'"

Greta's eyes widened and her cheeks paled. "What?"

"The voice of experience here. I had reservations before I married my ex, and I ignored the tiny voice in my head. I regretted my marriage almost immediately, but... it was too late."

Greta's face darkened. "Tracy? What—"

She raised a palm to forestall Greta's questions. "It's in the past. Cliff is dead, and I'm starting over. My point is simply to be sure the man you're marrying is the person you want to spend your life with. It's easy to get swept up in the wedding plans or the romanticism of a proposal and engagement, and shut out the doubts."

Jack's sister looked visibly shaken, and Tracy regretted having said anything. She may have had a bad marriage, but who was she to rain on Greta's parade? She ducked her head, ashamed of herself for her negativity. "Greta, forgive me. I shouldn't be such a downer. Just because I got into a bad situation doesn't mean I have the right to spoil your happiness."

Greta nudged her horse closer to Mabel so that she could put a hand on Tracy's arm. "Don't apologize for caring. You're absolutely right, and your frankness is refreshing." She squeezed Tracy's good wrist gently. "I hate that your marriage left you with scars, but...don't give up on the idea of love. Your prince is out there. I just know he is. You deserve someone who makes you happy." Greta shifted her hand back to the horn of her saddle and glanced out toward one of the pastures. "And you're right. Now is the time to think long and hard about what I want."

Movement in her peripheral vision pulled Tracy's attention to the stable yard, where a ranch hand in a black hat was checking the hooves of a gray horse. As the cowboy straightened from his task, he glanced toward the practice corral. Tracy's breath lodged in her throat as his eyes locked on hers.

Not a ranch hand. Jack.

He gave her a slow nod of greeting, and she twitched a smile, even as her heartbeat kicked up.

"Hmm."

Greta's hum of interest drew her attention, and she turned to see Jack's sister watching her with a knowing grin.

"What?" Tracy asked innocently, although the sting in her cheeks said her damnable tendency to blush gave her away.

Over the next several days, Tracy spent much of her time learning how to muck stalls, groom horses and feel more comfortable in the saddle. Her busy days learning ranch work left her exhausted at night, but the ache made her happy, made her feel productive and useful. She enjoyed working side by side with Seth as he did his chores and was amazed at how much the little boy knew about ranching. Not that she should be surprised, since Jack was such a good teacher.

True to his word, whenever she was around Seth, Jack was close by, keeping tabs on their conversation and interaction. At first she considered his hovering annoying, but before long, she found herself looking forward to Jack's presence as much as Seth's, but for wholly different reasons. Like a schoolgirl, she caught herself anticipating an accidental touch of their hands or an opportunity to spend time alone with Jack. She even looked for errands she could send Seth on to provide such one-on-one time with his father. And was it her imagination, or did Jack move closer to her, touch her more often and look into her eyes more deeply when Seth left them alone together?

On one occasion, when Jack sent his son to retrieve a pair of work gloves from his truck, she suspected Jack was using the same ploy. She'd even thought he might be ready to kiss her, when Seth scurried back into the stables shouting, "Hey, Daddy, your truck is locked."

Jack stepped back from her quickly and mumbled something under his breath. "Never mind, Spud. I'll get them later."

A couple of the ranch hands, a young fellow named Kurt Rodgers and an older, slightly pudgy man named Tom Vasquez, entered the stable then, sharing a laugh.

Tom slowed his step and gave Jack a funny look as they passed the stall where he and Tracy had been grooming Mabel. "Everything okay, boss?"

"Uh, yeah. Why?"

"Well, it just seems like you've been spending a lot more time than usual in the stable and pastures in the last few days. If we're not doing something right—"

"No." Jack raised a hand to reassure the man, and Tracy swore his cheeks flushed under his tan. "Y'all are doing fine. I just, um, wanted to show Tracy the ropes, you know?"

Tom flashed a knowing grin. "Oh, I think I know."

Kurt muffled a chuckle, and Jack shifted uncomfortably before asking, "Did Brett tell you two that the shipment of vaccines arrived? We'll start vaccinating the calves tomorrow."

Tom tugged on the brim of his hat. "Sure thing, boss. See ya, ma'am."

Tracy smiled and gave a little wave as they shuffled away.

"I want to help with the calves!" Seth said, bouncing on his toes.

"We'll see," Jack replied in the classic parental stalling technique.

But the next morning, Seth arrived at the main house just as Tracy was heading down to the ranch yard to see what she might help with today. Seth gave her a disgruntled pout and crossed his arms over his chest. "Daddy said I can't help with the calves getting shot."

"Shot?" Tracy echoed in shock, before she figured out his meaning. "Oh, getting their shots…the vaccines?"

He bobbed his head, frowning. "I'm big enough!"

"Well," she said, not wanting to contradict Jack, "for most things, but…I was hoping you'd take me on that walk you mentioned a few days ago."

Seth's face brightened. "I can show you the fishing pond and the old tree where Daddy made my tree house!"

When he grabbed for her hand and tugged, she laughed. "Now?"

"Sure! Why not?"

"Well…" She knew she needed to check with Jack before she disappeared with Seth into the surrounding fields. "I'll need to change shoes. These are my ranching boots, not my walking shoes." Nodding toward his bare feet, she added, "And you'll need to put shoes on."

He gave a negligent shrug. "I go barefoot all the time."

"Hmm. Just the same, if you're walking with me, I'd prefer your feet were protected."

He rolled his eyes as if she were the silliest female ever and groaned in capitulation. "Okay. Meet me at my house in a few minutes."

When he fetched a bicycle from the grassy lawn and pedaled away, she muttered, "I need one of those." Typically, she hitched a ride with Brett on a UTV for the two-mile stretch from the main house to Jack's home and the ranch's other outbuildings.

"Need what?"

She turned and smiled a greeting to Big J as he brought a glass of what appeared to be tomato juice out to the patio. Or perhaps a bloody Mary, she amended, noticing the celery stalk and ice cubes in his drink.

"I was coveting Seth's bike. Brett headed out early this morning, and I was dreading the walk down to Jack's house."

Her host chuckled and set his drink aside to reach in his pocket. "You're in luck. I have just the thing for you, darlin'."

Tracy slid her sunglasses to the top of her head as Big J pulled a ring of keys from his pocket. After flipping through the collection a moment, he wiggled one small key loose and dangled it on his index finger. "We keep a couple golf carts in the garage off the back wing of the house for Abra and the house staff to use as needed. This key works for the blue cart. Use it whenever you want for as long as you're here, my dear."

"Why, thank you!" She crossed the patio and took the proffered key. "That's very generous."

He pursed his lips. "Pshaw! You'll be doing me a favor. If they're not used regularly the batteries go bad, and Abra has no interest, most days, in going anywhere near the stables or other outbuildings."

Tracy repeated her thanks and hurried inside to change into more appropriate clothes for a walk. How would Jack feel about her going to the fishing pond with Seth? Was Jack going to be involved in vaccinating the calves?

If not, he'd likely insist on accompanying them. Secretly, she hoped he would, although the time alone with Seth would be welcome, too. She wanted to broach topics with Seth that she guessed Jack wouldn't approve of.

Ten minutes later she parked in front of Jack's house and tooted the tinny horn for Seth. As she climbed out of the golf cart, the boy burst through the front door, having donned a pair of tennis shoes.

When he skittered to a stop in front of her, she put a hand under the boy's chin to meet his eyes. "Is your dad home? Did you tell him where you were going?"

"He's working in his office. He doesn't mind me goin' places, s'long as I have an adult with me."

She twisted her mouth as if considering his assertion. "I think you should at least let him know where you're headed."

Seth rolled his eyes but trudged back to the house, opened the door and hollered, "Daddy, I'm goin' to the fishing pond with an adult!"

She heard a muffled reply from deep in the house, and Seth slammed the front door as he scampered back to join her. "Come on, I'll show you the shortcut!"

He took her hand and tugged her toward one of the pastures. She followed, jogging to keep up with the pace Seth set, and occasionally sidestepping to avoid cow patties. After crossing the pasture, Seth ducked through the fence and rambled into an area where a few trees dotted the landscape.

Tracy panted for a breath, winded from the sprint across the field. Pressing a hand to her racing heart, she gasped, "Seth, slow down! I thought…we were taking a walk! You've…done nothing but run…since we left the house."

"Oh." He curled his mouth in a sheepish grin. "Right. I forget old people can't run so good."

Tracy sputtered a laugh. "Who are you calling old?"

Seth's eyes twinkled devilishly. "You."

She scrunched her face in a mock scowl, swatting at him. "Why, you scamp! I'll show you who can run!"

Laughing, he took off with her at his heels. They darted through the trees until Seth pulled up short and pointed up in the branches of a large oak. "That's the tree house my daddy helped me build. Wanna go up in it?"

"Umm…" Tracy eyed the two-by-four wood scraps nailed in evenly spaced intervals leading to the platform fifteen feet up the tree. Under normal circumstances, navigating the homemade ladder would have been tricky for her. She'd never been especially athletic. But her sore muscles promised to make it even more challenging.

"It's easy," Seth said when she hesitated. "I'll show you." And off he went, clambering like a monkey up the wooden ladder to his tree house.

Not willing to let her cousin's boy down, especially when she had this rare opportunity to talk with him alone, she began an awkward ascent. One hand, one foot, hand, foot, hand, foot, achy muscles screaming, until she dragged herself into the fort next to Seth.

He grinned at her. "You did it!"

She cuffed him on the shoulder lightly. "You don't have to sound surprised." Even if she was a bit surprised at herself…and embarrassingly proud, as well.

He scooted to a window, cut from the sheet of plywood that comprised one of three walls, with the trunk of the oak making the bulk of the fourth wall. Peering out the window herself, she saw that the outside of the wooden walls had been reinforced with corrugated sheets of metal, spray painted with green-and-brown camouflage.

"Fancy." She flashed Seth an impressed look. "Very sturdy. And camouflaged, too?"

"Yep. It was my idea to paint the camo so it was hidden. Do ya like it?"

She hugged his shoulders and nodded. "It is the best tree house I've ever seen!"

Her opinion clearly pleased him, and he settled on the

small homemade wood bench that sat against one wall. "Did you ever have a tree house when you were a kid?"

She joined him on the tiny bench, suppressing a grunt as her leg muscles throbbed and her knees creaked. Though she felt battered and sore from her scalp to her toenails, she wouldn't trade this chance to visit with Seth for all the world or an ache-free body. "No. I grew up in an apartment in Denver. I didn't have a yard. If I wanted to play outside, I had to go to the park a few blocks from my building."

"No yard?" Seth gaped at her, his tone truly astonished.

"Afraid not. I'm a city girl through and through."

He wrinkled his nose as he mulled over this news. "Gosh, I'm glad I'm not a city boy. I love playin' outside and helpin' with the cows and horses."

"And from what I've seen, you are very good at it." She tweaked his nose, and he chuckled. "You'll make an excellent rancher when you grow up."

He puffed up his chest, and a broad grin spread across his face. He fell silent then and picked at the loose rubber at the toe of his muddy tennis shoe. "Ms. Tracy?" The quiet, almost reluctant pitch of his voice told her his thoughts had grown serious.

"Yes, sweetie?"

"Was my mom a city girl?"

Her pulse skipped. Jack's warnings about what she could and couldn't tell Seth about his mother echoed in her head. Her own resolve not to lie to Seth surged to the surface, and she drew a deep breath. "Sort of. She grew up in the suburbs."

He tipped his face up to hers. "What's a sub-burp?"

She sputtered a laugh. "Not burp. Burb. Suburb."

He laughed at his mistake, and predictably, because

he was a boy, he forced a burp. She pulled a face to show him she didn't find his belch funny, and he lowered his gaze in remorse.

Tousling his hair, she explained, "A suburb is a neighborhood close to a city. Your mom had a nice yard growing up, as I recall, but she was something of a girlie girl."

"What's a girlie girl?" He scooted closer to Tracy, soaking up what she told him like a sponge.

"She loved girlish things. She liked dolls and tea parties and dressing up in hats and jewelry."

He sneered. "Ew!"

"And her room was pink and frilly, and she had lots of Hello Kitty stuff and *Barbies*," Tracy said with relish, enjoying the way he cringed in disgust. "I loved to go to her house because we could play with her Barbie camper and her Barbie pool and her Barbie beauty shop…"

"Ugh!" He covered his head with his arms as if to deflect the girl cooties. "Stop!"

She tickled him under the arms. "What's the matter, Seth? Don't you like Barbies?"

"No! Barbies suck!"

She gasped at the harsh word that sounded all the more crude coming from a five-year-old's mouth. His eyes cut up to hers, and he wrinkled his nose in dread.

"Oops. Don't tell my daddy I said that, or I'll get in trouble."

She arched an eyebrow. "Where did you learn that word?"

"Daniel said it. But he said I couldn't or Daddy'd get mad." Seth's face sobered, and he grasped her sleeve. "You won't tell him, will you?"

She pursed her lips as if considering the matter. "Tell you what. If you promise never to say that word again, I'll keep this little slip as our secret. Deal?"

He released a big breath and smiled. "Deal." He wiggled around on the bench to face her. "Tell me more stuff about my mom."

Tracy's heart pattered. Here was the opening she'd been looking for. But now that she had the chance to talk to Seth about Laura, what should she say?